Behind the Blue

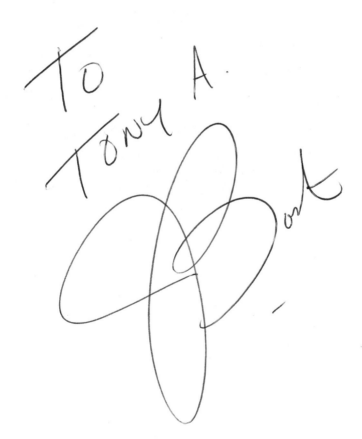

Behind the Blue

Joseph Bost

Library of Congress Control Number: 2009900929
ISBN: Hardcover   978-1-4415-0841-6
                     Softcover   978-1-4415-0840-9

To order additional copies of this book, contact:
Xlibris Corporation
1-888-795-4274
www.Xlibris.com
Orders@Xlibris.com
58259

To my parents, Madelyn and Charles.

And to my wife, Gina.

Thanks to my sister Judy, to my brother-in-law Joseph,
artist Charles V. Sabba, and to all those who inspired me to
finish.

Chapter 1

TONY STEPPED HARDER on the gas pedal. He was already doing sixty, twenty miles an hour over the speed limit on Route 88, his heart racing along with the revs of his engine. The speed limit was the last thing on his mind. It was late, and he had no idea of the time, nor did he care—he just wanted to get closer to home with his precious cargo. Even though the drive back from Manhattan only took thirty-five minutes, it seemed much longer. *Just one more stretch on Route 88 and I'll be home free,* he thought. Tony looked over at Vince who was staring out the passenger window, looking more nervous than excited. Tony's mind was busy calculating the numbers, making certain he was accurate. He couldn't stop thinking about the deal they had just made, which had gone far better than expected. In fact, it was the opportunity of a lifetime—the perfect score. Even as he sped along the road, he couldn't believe it. *If I could do one more deal like this one, I'd be set for life. And those Chinese, either they don't know what they're doing, or they have so much money they just don't know what to do with it,* Tony thought. He knew Dominick would be very pleased with him even if he "forgot" to tell him the entire truth. Dominick would never have expected the Chinks to pay 1.2 million dollars for thirty-five kilos of coke.

"Vince, you know what we have to do?" Tony said, looking straight ahead.

"Yeah, Tony, I know. How many times you gonna tell me?"

"Until you get your ass in the backseat and split up the money! We get two hundred thousand, and Dominick gets the rest, and don't forget to take the gun. We'll tell Dominick we sold the thirty-five kilos for a mil' and give back the extra four kilos."

"You sure you wanna do this? If Dominick ever finds out, you know what he'll do to us," Vince said, knowing it was useless to try changing Tony's mind.

"Are you kidding?" Tony said, raising his voice. "That fat bastard sits high in his multimillion-dollar mansion barking out orders like Don Corleone while we do all of his shit work. Look, Dominick told us not to take anything less than a mill for the thirty-nine kilos, otherwise, we were supposed to walk away, right? But we did better—an extra two hundred thousand and four kilos to spare. Do you really think he's going to miss a lousy two hundred K? After all, he's been hitting the coke a lot lately. I think we should do another deal with these stupid rich Chinks, take our cut, and start our own business."

Vince turned from the window and looked at Tony. It seemed that Tony was in his own world, looking straight ahead talking to himself, just rambling on, not giving a shit whether he was really listening.

A second later, Tony turned to meet Vince's gaze. "As soon as I turn off of 88, I'll stop on Kanes Lane. It should be deserted this time of night. Split the money, then we'll go to Dominick's."

Vince didn't like taking Dominick's money, but he knew Tony was going to take it no matter what he said or did. It was the most money he would ever see in his lifetime, so he went along with Tony even though he knew it would be a bullet in the back of the head if Dominick found out. There was no safe way out, so Vince nodded his head in agreement and didn't say a word.

Tony took out his cell phone, flipped it open, and quickly dialed a number with his right thumb. The call was answered immediately. "We're on our way back," he said. "The temperature was one Celsius, most of the snow has melted except for four inches."

"Good job. See you soon," replied the voice on the other end.

"Real soon," Tony said, a sly grin spreading across his face.

Vince looked at Tony blankly after Tony ended the call.

Tony chuckled to himself, impressed that it was his idea to use a code to inform them that they were returning with one million and four kilos.

Tony was twenty-five years old, a second generation Italian who grew up in the rough streets of New York. He came from a broken family, raised mostly by his aunt. By the age of fifteen, he dropped out of school thinking that burglaries and strong-arm robberies would be his new line of employment and a way to make fast money. A few months later, his new line of work ended abruptly when he was sentenced to three years in juvenile detention. When he hit the age of eighteen, he earned six years in the state prison for carjacking a vehicle in the parking lot of a Dunkin' Donuts store. Tony had positioned himself beside the drive-through window and waited for the woman to pay for her coffee. As she took her coffee and change from the employee at the window, Tony gestured at the woman through the passenger window as if he needed directions. When the woman lowered the window, he unlocked the door immediately and jumped inside. He pulled a handgun from his waistband and told the woman to drive around the corner of the building. Once she steered the car around the coffee shop, Tony grabbed the woman's coffee and told her to get out or he would shoot her. She jumped out, appropriately hysterical, and Tony sped out of the lot, only to be picked up fifteen minutes later by the authorities. He never realized that the coffee attendant witnessed the entire incident and called the police.

After six years in prison, still looking for the quick buck, Tony's prayers were finally answered when he was approached by an unexpected acquaintance who asked him to join the organization. He accepted without a second of hesitation. By this evening, Tony had been with the organization for a little more than a year. Vince was his passenger tonight, the newest member of the group, and Tony made sure Vince understood who was in charge.

Tony reached into his shirt pocket and slid out a small glass vial. Once he popped it open, he snorted another quick hit of coke. He mashed down a little harder on the gas pedal as the coke took his head and soul into the heavens. They would be there in no time.

Chapter 2

AT ABOUT THREE thirty in the morning on Sunday, August 4, Officer Joey Sabba was working the night shift, filling in for Jeff Urban who needed the night off. Joey was alone in his patrol car. Thanks to the shrinking budget, he had no partner. The mayor had pressured the chief to do away with two-man patrols; the same number of patrol cars, but fewer cops manning them. The workdays were eleven hours long, with four days on and two off. Every two weeks, the shift would rotate from nights to days, and the result was always chaotic. The changes were tough on the body, and the cops involved never were able to become accustomed to one set of hours. The night had been slow and was dragging by. Joey's eyes were getting heavy, so he drove to his favorite spot on Route 88 and parked.

Until they built Route 24, a four-lane thoroughfare that ran directly through Two River Township, 88 had been a busy two-lane highway. Route 88 was now used mostly by the locals who were in no hurry to get from one end of town to the other. At this time of night, the road was usually desolate.

As Joey sat in his car trying to stay awake, he saw a car speeding northbound just short of the bend. Giving in to his tiredness, he decided to give the speeder a break and let him go. But after the car sped around the bend and out of sight, he heard the unmistakable sound of a crash. The dangerous curve that snaked like a big S was well-known to most people, and just before, the speed limit dropped from forty to just fifteen miles an hour. For additional safety, a large illuminated yellow caution sign was posted on the shoulder that read DANGEROUS CURVE AHEAD. This was this section of road where the worst accidents occurred, and from the sound of it, Joey figured it was a bad one. Joey activated his overhead lights and siren and sped toward the collision.

About fifty yards down the road, Joey saw a pair of bright red brake lights shining from the rear of a car that had careened off the road and settled into a small engulfment. As he drove closer, he saw smoke billowing out from under the hood of the car. The front end of the vehicle was smashed like an accordion, stopped in its tracks by a huge oak tree. Joey pulled his cruiser behind the Jeep Cherokee, making sure to keep a safe distance and blocking the shoulder of the roadway to any oncoming traffic. He put his vehicle in park and immediately radioed headquarters.

"Car 14 to headquarters," Joey said into the mic.

"Come in, 14," replied the dispatcher, who had been watching the television and was annoyed that Joey was disturbing the silence with a car stop.

"Fourteen. I'll be out with an accident involving a vehicle that struck a tree at the curve on Route 88. The plate number is NJ registration XVY23W on a silver Jeep Cherokee. I'll let you know what I need."

"Received, 14."

Joey exited his vehicle and walked to the crushed Jeep. He pulled the flashlight from his belt and peered into the driver's side window. Inside he could see a body slumped over the steering wheel. The driver was the only one in the car, and he was not moving. He grabbed the door handle and tried to pull it open. He was able to crack it a couple of inches, but the door's hinge was jammed against the front fender. He yanked it again, the sound of metal grinding, the stubborn door only giving in a little more. He placed the flashlight on the ground and grabbed the side of the door with both hands, using all his strength; he wrenched it open. Inside, there was plenty of blood splattered on the front seat, and Joey donned a pair of surgical gloves that he pulled from a small pouch on his gun belt. He reached down and grabbed the driver's bloody left wrist that lay limp on his lap, and could not find a pulse. He then checked the carotid artery on the side of the neck but was unable to detect any sign of life. The driver's head was turned to the left, staring at Joey, resting on the top of a broken steering wheel. An empty stare, like shark eyes. The windshield had been smashed completely out of the car, and the driver had fragments of glass embedded on his forehead. Joey had been at the scene of many accidents, but he'd never seen a windshield that had been shattered like this one. The surrounding area was pitch-dark, and Joey sensed that something, or someone, was missing.

He walked around the vehicle to the passenger's side and observed a few traces of blood on the crumpled hood, as if someone had taken a paintbrush sopping with red paint and splattered it horizontally from the twisted frame of the windshield down the length of the hood. The streaks fanned out in a wider arc until it became obvious that they reached the huge tree and the mangled front fender. Joey followed the trail of blood with his flashlight that led beyond the tree. Joey's eyes followed the beam of light about fifteen feet beyond the tree, and his breath caught when he recognized what the flashlight had disclosed. It was little more than a pile of mutilated human flesh mixed with shredded clothing. He knew that if he were to look a little harder, he would find the dismembered parts lying close by. And just as he had the thought, he noticed the decapitated head lying several feet away from the pile of flesh. Joey immediately pressed the transmit button on his lapel mic.

"Fourteen. Send the first aid squad, the fire department, and the accident investigation team. This is a double fatality. It looks like the passenger was ejected on impact and died instantly."

"Received, 14," said the lieutenant, who had taken the radio from the dispatcher. "We are notifying the fire department, the first aid squad and medics. The accident investigation team will also be responding. Should we put Blue Star on standby?"

"Negative, lieutenant. No need for the helicopter. They both bought it."

"Received, 14. I have car 15 responding to help you out with traffic or anything else you might need."

"Code 5," Joey replied as he acknowledged receipt of the lieutenant's message.

Aside from waiting for the first aid squad and medics to arrive and secure the scene for the investigation team, Joey knew there was nothing else he could do for either victim. He returned to the car and peered inside. The driver was a white male in his twenties. His thick black hair was matted with the blood that still oozed from a gash on top of his head. The steering wheel had snapped in half, and the column was impaled in his sternum, which appeared to have collapsed his chest.

Joey leaned across the driver and removed the keys from the ignition, and he glanced around the inside of the Jeep for any clues that might tell him why the driver hit the tree. He saw no empty containers of alcohol in the vehicle; in fact, he didn't smell any alcohol. On the floor behind the front seat, Joey spotted a medium duffel bag, which he pushed to the side. He then looked underneath the driver's seat from the back to make sure he hadn't missed anything. He knew everyone would be arriving in the next couple of minutes and wanted to check out the vehicle before the AI team descended on it. Finding nothing, he was preparing to close the rear door when he took notice of the duffel bag. Joey slid the bag over and unzipped it, and his eyes widened as he pulled it open. He took a step back in disbelief. The bag was filled with money. He looked closer and noticed stacks upon stacks of hundred-dollar bills. Joey dug his hand deeper into the bag, finding one plastic bag and then another. He pulled out a total of three square plastic bags of white powder, and from his experience as a cop, it looked like he had found three kilos of cocaine or heroin. At the very bottom of the duffel bag, he pulled out a black 9 mm semiautomatic pistol. As if controlled by some outside force, Joey instinctively picked up the Jeep's backseat and placed the bags of powder and the gun on the floor, carefully replacing the seat on top of them. When he finished, he quickly pulled the duffel bag out of the vehicle and locked it in the trunk of his patrol car. Seconds after he stashed the money, Joey heard the sirens coming in his direction.

The first aid squad arrived first and set up spotlights on both sides of the road, and in a matter of minutes, the darkness had given way to man-made daylight. Joey's patrol car was blocking the northbound lane, and Joey directed the driver of the fire truck that had just arrived to block the southbound lane. Despite the absence of traffic, both lanes had to be shut down. The medics got to work quickly and checked the driver's vital signs, after which, they began the process of establishing a pronouncement for the medical examiner. The firemen stood by to make sure the Jeep was not leaking any slippery liquids onto the roadway that would make conditions hazardous for other vehicles. They were also in charge of locating and bagging all the pieces of the passenger and decontaminating the scene of all bodily fluids. The accident investigation team had also arrived at the scene and would be there the rest of the night, taking measurements, determining vehicle speed and the length of the skid marks, if any. The AI team was called to the scene only when serious injuries or fatalities were involved. Before they were finished, they would have reconstructed to find out the cause, and after they were finished, the Jeep would be towed to the headquarters and placed in the sally port until the investigation was completed. The families of the driver and passenger would have to be contacted, and the insurance company would need all the details of the accident. Joey knew the white powder would be found eventually and thought briefly about discovering it himself and getting all the credit, but quickly changed his mind. He figured it would be better to distance himself from the accident as much as possible.

As everybody was busy with their respective duties, Joey's backup, Tom Brougham arrived and pulled in behind Joey's cruiser. Tom got out of his car, looked around, and spotted his partner walking away from the crash and talking with a firefighter. Tom ran over immediately and interrupted the conversation.

"Joe, what a mess! Do you know how it happened?"

"That's what Chris and I were just talking about," Joey said, motioning to the firefighter. "You know Chris Jenkins, don't you?"

"Sure, I do," Tom said impatiently.

"It's hard not to know him, right? After all, he's been around longer than the both of us put together. I've heard that if he stays another few years, the fire department will have to install a handicap parking space for him in their parking lot," Joey said with a wry smile.

"Listen, guys, I have work to do," Chris said, his frown visible as he walked toward the fire truck.

"So what happened?" Tom said, turning his back toward Chris as he left.

Joey shrugged his shoulders. "He might have fallen asleep or was going too fast around the bend. There were no signs of drugs or alcohol when I checked the inside of the car."

"Did you toss it real good?"

"No," Joey said, "I've seen enough blood and body parts for one night."

"C'mon, Joe. Let's check it before the AI team gets to it."

Normally Joey would have eagerly assisted Tom, but not this time. "You go ahead, Tom, but I don't think you're going to find anything."

"I just want to make sure," Tom said as he made his way over to the Jeep.

It wasn't too much longer when Tom called Joey's name and waved him toward the car. Tom was bent down in the rear of the Jeep with the backseat up, pointing to three plastic bags of white powder and a gun.

"Look at that, Joe. Looks like three kilos. That's more dope than the entire narc squad confiscated in the last two years. Must be worth a lot of cash on the street. These guys must be serious dealers."

"Great job," Joey said with the most excitement he could muster. He patted Tom on the back and knelt down beside him and said in a low voice, "Thanks, partner, you saved me some embarrassment from the AI team. Thank God you found it before they did."

"Yeah," Tom said in agreement. "I couldn't imagine their heads getting any bigger than they already are."

As Joey stood up and started to walk away, Tom asked, "Do we know their names?"

"There's nothing with any name in the glove compartment or the middle console?"

"No," Tom said. "I checked all the front compartments, nothing. No insurance card, no registration, nothing."

"Headquarters checked ownership with Division of Motor Vehicles, and the registered owner is the Hilltop Corporation. It's leased. Check with the squad or medics, maybe they found a wallet on him."

"Yeah, right. But first, I'm going to check the rest of the Jeep."

"Okay," Joey said as he walked away, wanting his shift to end as soon as possible.

Joey's shift ended at seven in the morning, and he had no problem getting the duffel bag from the trunk of his patrol car to his personal car. Every cop carried all kinds of duffel bags containing workout gear or work-related equipment to and from headquarters, so he didn't appear suspicious at all as he removed the duffel bag from the patrol car and put it into his ten-year-old Saab. Even so, Joey made sure no one saw him remove the bag. He got home at around eight, parked in his garage, and left the duffel bag in the trunk.

Chapter 3

THE NEXT DAY, the entire department was buzzing about Tom Brougham finding three kilos of cocaine and a handgun. It was big news for the Two River PD, and the newspaper people and the local TV news media were all over it. The local newspaper ran an article about it on the front page.

TWO RIVER TIMES AUGUST 5

While investigating a fatal accident on Route 88 in Two River at 3:30 AM Sunday, Police Officer Tom Brougham discovered three kilos of cocaine under the rear seat of a Jeep Cherokee. The car had been driven by a white male who was accompanied by a white male passenger. Also found was a 9 mm handgun. Two River PD has not yet released the names of the deceased. Captain Grahill stated that the accident is still under investigation and that he could not release any further information at this time.

The article went on to discuss the importance of stopping drugs and taking the drug dealers off the street, putting them behind bars, and describing how drugs affect children and are getting into the school systems. In fact, it continued for another half page, listing statistics that described how many young children are experimenting with drugs at an early age.

The local TV station, Local News 4You, interviewed Officer Brougham inside of headquarters. Tom was standing beside a small table on which the three bags of white powder and the 9 mm pistol had been placed. When the reporter asked a question, the camera would close in on Brougham's face, and as he answered, the view would shift to the small table and scan its contents. The interview lasted ten minutes, and News 4You said that it would be on channel 12 that evening.

Chapter 4

JOEY COULDN'T SLEEP. He felt a combination of fear and exhilaration as he thought about the money in the duffel bag. After three hours of tossing and turning, he got up and drove to the Atlantic Highlands marina, where he kept his thirty-foot sailboat. It was afternoon, not quite one o'clock, and the two slips on either side of his boat were empty. It was a hot, sunny August day, and everyone who had the time and money were on their boats either fishing or just having a good time. Joey opened the trunk of his car, grabbed the duffel bag, and headed for the sailboat. He untied the lines and motored slowly toward the Shrewsbury River to his favorite spot along the west bank. It was a small hidden spot behind a small peninsula of federally owned land that twisted and curved to hide the small pier nestled into its armpit. Joey loved the area because it was known only by the locals and remained safely hidden from the part-time bennys, the weekend boaters from Bronx, Elizabeth, Newark, New York, Staten

Island, who came from their wealthy towns to cause havoc on the water. None of them ever seemed to know anything about the proper etiquette of boating.

Joey grew up in Atlantic Highlands and has been sailing with his dad since he was a kid, so he knew every inch of the Shrewsbury and Navesink Rivers. Now forty-five years old, he still enjoyed sailing and being close to the beach. He kept his six-foot athletic frame in good shape by running the hills in Hawthorne Woods or cycling the fourteen-mile loop around Sandy Hook. His wavy black hair complemented his good looks and confident aura. As Joey coaxed the boat around the peninsula and headed toward the riverbank, the water became smooth as glass, and he spotted the tip of the pier that was protected by the outstretched arm of land. Fortunately, it was deserted. The tide was heading back out to sea, and the water was becoming more shallow. His sailboat needed only four feet of water before it ran aground, which was a good thing because the changing conditions would make it impossible for the larger motorboats to get close to his favorite hideaway. They would have to remain in the channel, which was a couple hundred yards from the peninsula. Joey had not been to the pier in a long time, several years in fact, and as he pulled up and threw a line around an old piling, he was hit with a flood of nostalgia. Memories of his childhood, such as his high school days, when he got laid for the first time, got drunk with his friends for the first time, and even smoked his first joint. *If this pier could only talk, he'd be in big trouble*, he thought. He smiled to himself as the memories danced through his mind, but none of them displaced the overwhelming thought about the money that was down below. He couldn't help but think that, somehow, the universe had finally paid off and made him a wealthy man.

Once he'd tied the boat to the pier, Joey ducked inside the cabin, grabbed a beer from the small fridge, and unzipped the duffel bag. His heart raced, and his palms were moist with sweat.

"Calm down," he said out loud as he emptied the duffel bag on a small table in the galley.

Joey turned the bag upside down, and the stacks of money spilled out–as did another plastic bag of cocaine buried at the bottom. He realized immediately that he must have missed it during his cursory search. Joey pulled on a pair of gloves and set the drugs aside. In front of him lay a huge pile of money, the most he had ever seen. He couldn't help remembering two years ago when he had bought his condo.

Inside the attorney's office, as he was signing stacks of papers, the lawyer handed him a check made out to Joseph Sabba for two hundred thousand dollars, which was the amount of his mortgage.

"Enjoy the moment," he'd said, "this is probably the most money you will ever hold in your hand at one time."

Joey laughed to himself and thought, *Looks like you were wrong.* Right now, there was a lot more money in front of him. He counted a hundred and twenty stacks of hundred-dollar bills that were bound with paper wrappers about an inch wide. He counted one of the stacks of hundreds, which totaled ten thousand dollars. Joey did a fast calculation, and if each of the stacks was worth ten thousand dollars, then his net worth had just increased by 1.2 million dollars.

His mind began to run wild. He could retire from work, buy a bigger sailboat and sail it around the world. Trade in that old Saab for a new Lexus. Or he could move to Vieques, a little island off the coast of Puerto Rico, where the cost of living was cheap, but he was still in a US territory. In either case, he'd never have to work another night shift. *The hell with the department,* Joey thought. He gave them the best years of his life, did a good job, and still they never promoted him to sergeant. He put his life on the line every day so everyone else could feel safe going about their everyday business. The average businessman goes to work wearing a nice suit armed with nothing but a hundred-dollar Montblanc pen in his shirt pocket. He had to go to work wearing a bulletproof vest under his police shirt and a gun on his hip, hoping to return home safe at the end of the day. Joey thought about the people who lost their lives on September 11, all those cops and firefighters who died. While everyone else was running away from the blazing towers, the police and firefighters were running toward them, trying to save people's lives, only to lose their own, all for a lousy seventy grand a year. It seemed ironic to Joey that a drug dealer could ride around in his car with more than a million dollars' worth of drugs and money and treat it like loose change. Joey wanted a piece of the good life.

Now Joey could tell his chief to go screw himself, throw his badge and gun on the desk, and just walk out. He didn't need the job, the headaches, or the stress. Joey opened another beer and tried to relax after he realized that he was working himself up for no reason. He had to control himself, and self-control was no stranger to him. Joey was disciplined, smart, and knew he couldn't even think about touching the money for six months to a year. In the meantime, he'd hide it and go to work each day as if he never hit the lottery. Satisfied with his decision, he tucked the money neatly, lovingly into the duffle bag, and his eyes followed the zipper all the way across as he pulled it closed. He placed the bag inside a tiny hidden compartment underneath the spot where his anchor was stored. He pushed on the small brass knob on the hatch, making sure it was securely shut. He looked at the knob knowing that it hadn't been polished since Tina was here with him last. Joey turned and stepped up the narrow teak ladder and emerged onto the deck that was awash in the midafternoon sun. He stretched out on the deck, the sun blanketing his body, not wanting the euphoric feeling to leave. He did not feel this good in a very long time. The best he felt since his divorce two years ago, when his wife of ten years, Tina, left him for another man. Two years ago, Tina angrily told Joey she was going to see her mother in California during Christmas and would be home on New Year's Eve. She claimed that he always had to work the holidays and she was fed up with it. She hated the cop job and told Joey constantly that he should quit and do something better with his life. Joey tried to explain that the benefits and the pension were too good to give up and that he would be able to retire when he turned fifty. But Tina usually answered the same way, over her shoulder, as she stormed away mad.

"It's twenty-five years out of your life, Joey, not mine." It had been the third time she went to California to see her mother that year, and Joey knew she and her mother had never been close. In preparation for her return, Joey had planned a special New Year's Eve party for Tina at his friend's restaurant, Lana's, over in Clark Township. But late that afternoon, Tina called and told him, in a nonchalant tone as if talking about the weather, that she was not happy with the marriage and wanted a divorce. She explained that she had met someone in California and would let him know when she would come home to get her things. Joey couldn't speak, stunned at what he was hearing. He flipped the phone shut and threw it against the living room wall, smashing it into pieces. He collected all the pictures of the two of them that he could find and threw them in the garbage. He then emptied out her bedroom closet. Filled up three huge storage boxes with her clothes and threw them in the garage and later dumped them into a charity clothes drive box. If he had a fireplace, he would have burned them. He should have taken the advice of his best friend who was against the marriage. Even his mother was opposed to it. She had a unique way of getting her point across and said to him one day when she found out he was getting married, "Remember, Joey, love is blind, but the neighbors ain't." Fortunately, there were no children. The only thing they had to split was their two-bedroom condo in Atlantic Highlands. In the divorce agreement, she received a hundred thousand dollars in cash, which was all of Joey's savings, and he got to keep the condo and his entire pension. It took Joey a long time before he could start to lose his hurt and anger.

Joey caught himself daydreaming and decided that this was definitely not the time to think about the past. Now it was the future that counted. Soaking in the sunshine, Joey closed his eyes and tried to think of the future, but his mind wouldn't cooperate. Suddenly, it took him back to the time he made love to his high school sweetheart on the pier of Pirate's Cove many years ago. It was his last thought before he dozed off.

Chapter 5

IT WAS SIX o'clock, and Dominick's seventy-inch plasma was tuned to the evening News 4You on channel 12. He sat in his big leather chair, puffing on a Don Carlos Presidente, eager to get a look at the cop who investigated the accident–and had found his cocaine and money. The only thing mentioned in the newspapers was the three bags of cocaine, but there was nothing about the money. If the police had the money and the coke, it wouldn't be such a big deal. After all, things like this were bound to happen, especially in Dominick's business. It was human error, which is never figured into the equation. Too bad Tony had to die in that accident. He would have enjoyed giving Tony a very slow and painful death for being so reckless with his property. Tony would never have made it to trial. Dominick suddenly lost all interest in Tony and now concentrated on the face of Tom Brougham, the police officer on the news who was giving a step-by-step account of the accident and how he found the cocaine. It sounded like the accident had gotten more dramatic as time went on. Tom gave an accurate account of what happened, leaving out any part in which he was not included. Joey's name was never mentioned, nor was the money. Dominick picked up his cell phone and punched in the ten-digit phone number from memory. After two rings, a voice answered.

"Are you watching the channel 12 news?"

"Yes," replied the receiver.

"Good. I want to know everything about this cop–where he lives, the car he drives, and what he does in his private life. I want to know everything about the accident–where it happened, when it happened, and who was out there first."

"Okay," said the voice on the other end.

Dominick slammed the phone shut and motioned to Michael Power, who stood to his right side. Michael walked over, knowing what Dominick was about to say. "I'll have all the information you need by tomorrow. Take your time, and do what you have to. I want my million dollars," Dominick said.

Chapter 6

THREE DAYS HAD passed since the accident, and by now, it was barely mentioned by the other officers in the department. It had already become old news. Tom had his fifteen minutes of fame with his name in the newspaper and an interview on channel 12. His wife and two kids were very proud of him. His oldest son, Jason, was in the eighth grade, and all his friends in school thought his dad was a supercop who should be on *The Shield*. His daughter, Nicole, was only five, but she got very excited each time she saw her daddy on television—as long as he didn't interfere with SpongeBob. Tom was tired of the everyday routine, dealing with people's problems, barroom brawls, drunk drivers, and domestic disputes, but finding the cocaine boosted his morale for a couple of days. Yet the third day after that morale boost, Tom began to notice a car following him. He wasn't positive, but he thought he'd seen the same car four times within two hours while he was out running errands. The car stayed at a safe distance, which made it impossible for him to get the plate number or a description of the driver. The car was a newer model, black Chevy Blazer. Its presence bothered him, but he didn't get rattled until the fourth day when he received a call on his cell phone. Tom was in the den, sitting in his favorite lounge chair reclined all the way back, enjoying a quiet moment while Judy and the kids were out food shopping. The Yankees were on the TV beating Oakland by ten runs, and Tom started to doze off when his cell phone rang. He checked the incoming call that read restricted on his caller ID. He flipped open the phone and said hello.

"Give us our money, and your family will not be harmed. We are watching you." The line went dead immediately afterward.

Tom had no idea what was going on. *Who was that asshole?* A prank call maybe, or it might be someone he locked up recently who was busting his balls trying to get even. The thing Tom despised was that the caller threatened his family. If the asshole had a beef with him, then keep it between the two of them.

Two days later, Tom received another phone call, and this time it was on the house phone. His wife, Judy, answered the kitchen phone while she prepared peanut butter and jelly sandwiches for the kids. Tom was in the garage fixing a flat tire on Jason's bike when Judy yelled to him that he had a phone call. A minute later, Tom entered the kitchen, wiping his hands clean with a paper towel and grabbed the phone.

"Hello?"

After a second, the voice said, "Smart of you to turn in the cocaine, but not too smart of you to keep the money. Be at Harbor Park at ten o'clock tomorrow night. Bring the money." The line went dead. Tom hung up the phone and had a worried look on his face. A look Judy knew well. When something went wrong at work, Tom would come home distant and quiet, taking days to communicate to her what bothered him. She had learned years ago to give him his space and eventually he would open up.

"Who was that, Tom? Is everything okay?" Judy asked, concerned.

Tom checked his expression and forced himself to relax. "Everything's fine. Something came up at work, is all. Nothing important. I'll be back in a little while, hon." He kissed her and left the house.

Joey was on his sailboat, which was still docked at the marina, and Tom knew where to find him on his off days in the summer. Tom was glad to see his sailboat still in the slip. Joey was with a beautiful young girl who looked no older than twenty-five. She was wearing a bikini that was so skimpy it barely covered her large breasts. Both were on deck sitting in the sun, sharing a bottle of champagne when Tom arrived.

"What are you celebrating?" Tom asked as he walked up to the boat, unable to look away from the small bikini stretched out in front of him.

Joey smiled and raised his glass at Tom. "What's there not to celebrate? It's a beautiful day, I'm with a beautiful woman, and I'm off from work. By the way, this is Michelle."

Tom gave Michelle a quick smile and then looked back at Joey. "You're in a very festive mood today."

"Every day away from the department is a good reason to be celebrating. What brings you here? Bored with your celebrity status and need a little excitement?" Joey glanced in Michelle's direction, who happened to be his flavor of the week.

"I need to talk to you about something . . . about the accident."

"Always talking about work," Joey said, grinning. "Why don't you come aboard? We'll go for a ride around Manhattan. It's a beautiful day. I promise I'll have you back in a couple of hours."

"No, not today. I can't. I just need to talk to you," Tom said, with urgency in his voice.

"No problem, Tom. Look, I need to take care of a little business first. Why don't we meet at the Quay in Sea Bright–say five o'clock–for a bite to eat? It's on me. I plan on working up an appetite." He added a quick wink for good effect.

"Okay, I'll see you at five," Tom said. He left to go home and take his daughter, Nicole, to her music lesson.

Chapter 7

JOEY RETURNED FROM his pleasure cruise at half past three and promised Michelle they would do it again real soon. He said good-bye with a kiss and watched her ass sway side to side as she walked through the parking lot toward her car. *What a body, too bad she doesn't have a brain to match,* Joey thought. Still, one hour of meaningless conversation followed by two hours of great sex was the perfect ratio. After two orgasms, Joey wished the girl would turn into a Grey Goose martini and a good cigar. He laughed out loud and then went down into the cabin to shower.

Joey arrived early at the Quay and ordered a martini at the bar. He took a seat that gave an unobstructed view of the Shrewsbury River and enjoyed the air-conditioning, especially after being in the sun all afternoon. Ordinarily, Joey would be taking in the beautiful view, watching all the different-sized boats go by as the bright sun descended toward the west. But even though he was staring out the window, the view was all but forgotten. Instead, he was thinking about Tom and what he'd wanted to talk about. Joey was positive that no one had seen him take the money, and his name was never associated with the accident. Maybe Tom just wanted to apologize for not giving him any credit for being the first one on the scene and discovering the accident. Whatever the case, Joey had the money. It was his. No one knew he had it, and no one was going to take it away. With the right investments, at 8 percent, 1.2 million dollars would give him a return of ninety-six thousand every single year–for doing nothing but getting out of bed. When the time was right, Joey would hire the best tax lawyer he could find and invest overseas. The IRS would never have a clue about his income. He could put the money in an offshore account in the Cayman Islands, where the US government had no jurisdiction. The money he made would be all his, but he would lose Uncle Sam as a greedy partner. He would only have to pay taxes on his pension, assuming he finished his twenty-five years. He could retire now with twenty years of service and get 50 percent of his current salary, or stick around for the next five years and collect 65 percent. Whatever the case, thanks to the money, he could make that decision at any time.

Tom walked in at exactly five o'clock and sat on the stool next to Joey. Tom ordered a Coors Light, and Joey motioned for the bartender to put it on his tab. When Tom had his drink, Joey raised his martini glass and tapped Tom's bottle of beer.

"To good friends."

Tom nodded in agreement and took a quick sip of his beer as he tried to put the right words together. He'd known Joey for fifteen years. Since his divorce, they didn't socialize as much off the job as they used to, but they spent a lot of time together on the job.

"You missed a good time," Joey said. "I think Michelle liked you. She has a thing for cops."

"I'm sure you and what's-her-name did all right without me. I don't think Judy would have appreciated me going for a boat ride when our daughter needed to be at a music lesson."

Joey respected Tom's dedication to his family and decided to drop the subject.

"So what's so important about the accident that couldn't wait till I saw you at work?" Joey asked.

Tom looked intently down at his bottle of beer and, after a few moments, said, "A couple of days after the accident . . . I know this sounds strange . . . but I think I was being followed. Plus I received two phone calls, one on my cell phone and one at home. I believe it was the same person. The caller said that he would come after my family if I didn't give him the money. He also said something like, it was smart to turn in the cocaine, but not smart to keep the money. He told me to meet him at ten tomorrow night at Harbor Park, and he said to bring the money. I have no idea what's going on."

Joey's shoulders tensed up immediately, and he turned his head to stare across the bar as if taking in the view, trying to bide time and slow his heart rate, not wanting Tom to sense his nervousness. Joey slowly took a couple of deep breaths, trying to channel his anxiety and control his nerves. He turned to Tom and said, "You know we put a lot of people in jail and have made a couple of enemies along the way. Maybe it's one of these scumbags fucking with you."

"I thought of that, but how did he get my cell and home phone numbers?"

"Do you remember that cop from Lincroft? It was in the newspapers last year. His name was James Boyle, a sergeant."

"No, I don't remember," Tom said.

"Well, a friend of mine knows Sergeant Boyle, and he told me the whole story. Somehow, someone managed to get Boyle's address, social security number, and his date of birth. The guy had a fake driver's license and a fake birth certificate made using Boyle's name. The guy–I think his real name was Jon Conner–was from some hick town in Maryland. This guy Conner goes joy riding and accumulates all kinds of traffic tickets with his fake license, which go unpaid. This happens for months, and Sergeant Boyle winds up with a bunch of outstanding warrants for his arrest in three states. Unknown to Boyle, he's been the victim of identity theft. He drives his family to Florida and gets pulled over for speeding in North Carolina. The North Carolina state trooper checks his license and sees five thousand dollars in unpaid traffic tickets. The cops down there don't want to know anything. The trooper tells Boyle to put his badge back in his pocket and places him under arrest. It takes Boyle two days to get out of jail. The Lincroft PD had to fly one of their captains down to Maryland to identify Boyle and take care of the matter. To make things worse, when Boyle gets home, he looks at a credit report from one of the credit agencies and finds five credit cards with charges totaling ten thousand dollars–purchases he never made."

Joey continued, "Listen, Tom, anybody with a computer and the Internet can find anything about anyone. Just because you're a cop doesn't mean you're exempt. This asshole probably read about the accident in the newspaper, saw you on TV, and is screwing with you. It's someone you probably locked up."

"I hope so . . . it's just that I don't like them threatening my family."

"How much money are they talking about?"

"I don't know. The caller never mentioned an amount. He hung up before I had a chance to talk."

"And you said you were being followed?" Joey asked, taking a small sip of his martini, feeling a knot starting to build deep in his stomach.

"Yeah, I think so. The other day, I was out shopping at a couple of different places, and each time I went to a store, I saw the same black Chevy Blazer parked on a side street a block away. It was far enough away that I couldn't get a plate number or get a look at the driver."

"How did you know it was the same Blazer?"

"I wasn't convinced the first two times I saw it, but the third time, I noticed that the Blazer had a dent on the right front fender. On my last errand, I was getting into my car at the Home Depot, and I saw the Blazer with the dent parked by the exit. When I backed out of my parking space, it drove away."

"Were there any passengers?"

"One," Tom said, sipping his Coors Light.

"Did you mention this to anybody else?" Joey asked.

"No, no one knows. Not even Judy."

Joey's eyes narrowed, the knot in his stomach twisted tighter, and he felt like a golf ball was stuck in his throat. Joey forced out the words and said, "I'll go with you tomorrow to Harbor Park. We'll see if this guy is for real. They probably didn't realize you knew they were following you. Tomorrow night, if the Blazer is there, we'll get a plate number and find out who it is. After that, we'll make their lives miserable. We are the cops, after all."

"Are you okay?" Tom asked.

"I'm fine. Too much sun this afternoon, that's all," Joey said, clearing his throat and taking a sip of his martini.

For the first time, Tom had leaned back on his stool and looked out toward the river, appearing to be a little more relaxed and said, "I have an uneasy feeling about this whole thing. I should probably tell the patrol captain about the threats and have them documented just in case something really did happen to my family."

Joey picked up his martini glass to eye level and watched the sun's rays reflect through the clear vodka. He slowly took a large sip and placed the glass back on the napkin. He ran both his hands through his thick black hair, wiping away a couple small beads of sweat that accumulated on the top of his forehead, and turned his head toward Tom and said, "Trust me, it'll be all over by tomorrow night. Telling the captain will only make matters worse, especially with all his questions."

"Maybe you're right, but after tomorrow, if things go south, I'm going to the captain."

"Don't worry, it won't," Joey said.

"One more thing," Tom said, peeling the Coors Light label off his beer bottle. "Not that this is important, but the chief called me into his office yesterday, asking questions about the accident."

"What kind of questions?" Joey asked.

"The same questions that have been asked before. All the answers to the questions were in the police reports. I had a feeling that he was trying to read my body language, trying to see what my reactions were to certain questions."

"Which question was that?" Joey asked, feeling his heart rate accelerate.

Tom took one last drink from the bottle and drained it, producing an aah after he finished. He sat the bottle on the wet napkin in front of him and absently grabbed a couple of peanuts from the dish beside it. "He asked who was on the scene first."

"And," Joey prompted.

"I told him you were."

Joey worked hard to keep his heart rate down. He knew the chief was always looking for the negative. But why ask the questions? What was he looking for? Joey could feel the beads of sweat forming on his brow and hoped they weren't showing yet.

Tom popped a few more nuts into his mouth. "Yeah, and then he asked how long you had been there before I arrived."

Joey sat, dead quiet, and waited.

Tom shook his head a bit and shrugged his shoulders. "I told him I didn't know."

"You should have told the narcissistic prick to read my first responder report." Joey said, shaking his head in disgust.

"I don't put any credence into what the chief says. I just thought it was strange that he called me into his office to ask those questions when he already knew the answers."

"That's why they call him Reinus the Anus," Joey said. "I'll give Ann a call to see if she knows what's going on. It's good to have the chief's secretary as a personal friend for more than eight years."

Tom pushed back from the bar, but not before he'd refilled his palm with peanuts and said, "I have to be getting home, those phone calls I received keep playing in my head"–he paused for a moment, throwing the peanuts back into the bowl, wiping the palm of his hand on his pant leg, a concerned looked blanketing his face–"If anyone comes close to hurting my family, I'll–"

"Relax, Tom. Nobody is going to bother Judy and the kids. I told you, we'll find out tomorrow who they are, and it'll be over. Go home, tuck the kids into bed, and make love to your wife," Joey said, cutting him off. Joey leaned over and placed his right arm around Tom's shoulders.

Joey felt Tom's shoulders stiffened, and Tom turned away to get off his stool. Tom stood, faced Joey, and said, "You were the first one on the scene, do you think someone else could have gotten to the accident before you? Maybe somebody else drove by, pulled over to help, saw a bunch of money in the Jeep, and left prior to you getting there?"

Joey looked up and gazed out the window as if in deep thought, pondering the question. "I've been on the job for over twenty years, and I've seen some bizarre things go down. You have too, especially when it comes to greed and money. It's a possibility, I guess. I really don't know how long the Jeep was there when I found it."

Tom nodded his head slowly. "Thanks for listening, you've always been there for me. See you tomorrow," Tom said as he left.

Joey sat in deep thought. He ordered another martini in an attempt to numb his brain. He hated the fact that he lied to his partner. He had no problem keeping the money; after all, it was dirty money–it belonged to a drug dealer. If he had never taken the money, if it had been turned in with the kilos of dope, the money would just have been sucked back into the local and county governments for the politicians to spend. Maybe he should tell Tom what happened? Split the money with him? He could definitely use it. Joey reached down and lifted the plastic stirrer from his martini, with three huge olives speared through their center. He slipped one in his mouth and washed it down with a big gulp. Tom would never go along with it. Even if he did, Judy would find out eventually, then the kids, and then they'd both be in jail. He sat there and finished his drink. The alcohol and the afternoon sun had taken their toll, and he felt tired. He knew that what he needed was a good night's sleep. He would deal with his partner's problem tomorrow.

Joey was looking forward to getting to bed early and alone. He made it to his condo, which was only a five-minute drive from the Quay. The car seemed like it was on automatic pilot when he turned into his driveway and parked. Joey walked to the front door and pushed the key into the lock. As he did, the door slid open. He knew the door was locked when he left. There were no pry marks on the door or damage to the lock. He reached for his cell phone, flipped it open, and started to dial 911 and then stopped and put the phone back into his pocket. Since taking the money, Joey started to carry his off-duty Beretta. He took out his keys, locked the dead bolt on the front door, removed his gun from the holster, and quickly walked around the house and checked for a broken or an open window. Satisfied, he went straight to the rear door, knowing what he would find. The rear door, secured with a cheap lock, had been pried open. *The usual MO,* he thought, in through the rear and out through the front. He slowly pushed open the door, his gun drawn, pointed straight ahead. He entered the dimly lit kitchen and listened for any noise. Every cabinet door was opened, and pots and pans were scattered on the floor. He walked into the living room, the furniture had been turned upside down, and the cushions were slashed open—the fluffy white stuffing strewn about the room. He slowly turned in each direction, fanning his weapon, checking every corner. After checking the closet and bathroom, he climbed the steps to the second floor that lead to the bedrooms. He stopped at the top of the stairs; every picture frame had been ripped off the hallway walls. Gun pointed, he entered his bedroom. The wooden dresser drawers had all been yanked out, the contents scattered on the carpet. The closet door was ripped off the hinges, and all his clothes and police uniforms were piled on the floor. Joey went immediately into the second bedroom that served as an office, and he was relieved to see that his important papers were still in the filing cabinet. The shoe box that contained his grandfather's old coin collection had been opened, but all looked to be undisturbed. Even his gold jewelry and Rolex watch that he kept on a small side table next to his bed were still there. Joey had investigated many burglaries in his career, and most of them were done by local thieves looking for a quick dollar. Whoever it was had pried open the single lock and was able to get in easily. Joey had always preached to the victims of a burglary that they should install a security alarm and have a dead bolt put on every exterior door. Joey had neither; he made a mental note to put those two items on his to-do list, which was getting longer by the minute. He was tempted to call the police and make a formal report, but deep down inside, his gut feeling was that whoever broke into his house was looking for something in particular–a duffel bag full of money.

The condo was in disarray, and Joey was in no mood to start cleaning up. He was tired and needed some sleep. He secured the rear door as best he could and drove to the marina to sleep on his sailboat.

On the way to the marina, his mind was spinning. All kinds of questions were popping up. *What would tie them to me? Why are they searching my house? They were only looking for one thing. All my valuables were untouched. No one knew I was involved, not even the other cops. The media never mentioned my name. The only people that would know I was at the accident were the ones who actually read the police reports, and they were kept confidential. But the most important question was, who the hell are* they?

It was dark at the marina, and all the boats were in their slips. Joey could hear loud voices and laughter coming from some of the larger boats in the distance as he walked along the pier to his boat. He needed a few hours of sleep and hoped that his brain would allow him the pleasure. He tried to clear his mind by controlling his breathing through meditation, a technique he used to practice in yoga class with his ex-wife. He went straight to his cabin, but it took an hour of restless tossing and turning before he finally fell asleep.

At five in the morning, Joey awakened to the voices of a group of fishermen walking by, laughing, telling stories, and pushing a plastic marina wheel barrel, the sound of its wheels thumping across the wooden planks of the dock, filled with coolers and fishing poles in preparation to go catch their share of fluke. When he finally opened his eyes, his mind immediately flashed back to his partner's conversation and the break-in at his condo. The questions were coming back slowly. He got up, felt a little hangover, and realized he needed to go outside and get some fresh air. The inside of the cabin was starting to get hot and humid. He walked through the cabin and noticed a couple of things that were out of place. The storage cabinet behind the steps was open, and the safety vests had been moved. Also, a large built-in drawer underneath the couch had been pulled open and rummaged through. Joey headed up to the bow immediately to check the little anchor compartment. He yanked at the door and discovered with great relief that the duffel bag was right where he'd left it.

It was getting close to six o'clock already. Normally, Joey would be in his glory as he watched the sun start to peek above the horizon. Intrinsically, he knew it was a beautiful sight, but every day since he'd gotten his hands on the money, his life had become more complicated. Tom was being followed, and the security of his own life was being violated. It was something he could not allow to happen. Joey figured that he had two options. First, he could meet with the Blazer people and give back the money, just be done with it. Otherwise, he could skip the meeting and find out who the Blazer belonged to, figure out if they were a group of local thugs or possibly were involved with a New Jersey or New York crime family. If it was the latter, he would give the money back in a hurry. If it was the former, he could deal with them himself. So he decided that he would find out whose money he had. The first person he would start with was the registered owner of the Jeep Cherokee, the Hilltop Corporation.

Chapter 8

JOEY WENT TO see Detective Sergeant Kevin Sherman, who was second in charge of the department's twenty-member narcotics squad. Joey walked down the hall, along the beige cinder block walls, lit by the overhead fluorescent lights. He stopped in front of an office door with a brown placard that read in white letters, Detective Sergeant Sherman. He could hear a voice coming from inside the office, relieved that Sergeant Sherman was inside. Joey knocked on the door.

"Come in," yelled the voice from inside the room.

Joey entered the small, eleven-foot-square office, and Kevin motioned to him to sit in one of the two chairs in front of his desk. In over twenty years, this was the first time Joey had been in his office. Joey hated being inside the building. He preferred to be outside in his patrol car, which he called his office on wheels. Joey looked around and saw a framed eight-by-ten picture of Kevin's wife and with their two children, Billy and Kaitlyn. The wall behind the desk was decorated with numerous framed certificates, letters of recognition, and several photos of Kevin and members of his squad. There was a picture of Kevin shaking hands with the mayor, and another with the chief. But one picture in particular caught Joey's attention. It was an eight-by-ten of Kevin, the chief, the chief's secretary, Ann, and Dominick Zarza. All were dressed in suits, and Ann was wearing a black cocktail dress covering her small, five-foot frame; the picture reminded him that he needed to call Ann. Kevin and Dominick were both holding up some certificates and smiling for the camera. Kevin said good-bye to the caller and hung up the phone. Kevin was tall, good-looking with premature gray hair.

"Hi, Joe. How are you?" Kevin said, standing up and reaching out with his right hand.

"I'm fine," Joey said, shaking Kevin's hand.

"Fine?" Kevin repeated. "Do you know what fine really means?" Kevin asked, raising his tone slightly.

"I didn't know I was going to be quizzed when I walked in," Joey said, not knowing where this was going.

"I just completed a two-week FBI school in Quantico, Virginia, a week ago," said Kevin.

"So what? The chief went too, and it didn't do him any good. He's still dead between the ears," Joey said, smiling.

"Well, you can't change a zebra's stripes, you know. But I did learn a thing or two in one of their criminal psychological behavioral classes. Which brings me back to the question of *fine*. Did you know that when someone says they are fine, what they are really saying is they're Fucked up, Insecure, Neurotic, and Evasive?" Kevin grinned. "So you see, I just learned a lot about how you are doing today."

"You're a damn genius, Kevin. Did they also teach you how to read body language?" Joey said as he lifted his right hand and extended his middle finger.

"No, the FBI didn't have to teach that one, I learned that very early on in my career dealing with all the scumbags on the street." Kevin said as he finally sat at his desk.

Joey followed and took a seat in front of Kevin's desk. "Speaking of scumbags, did you find out anything else about the driver and passenger of the Jeep that crashed?"

"The two fatals where your partner found the coke?" Kevin asked, as if there was another to choose from.

"That's the one," Joey said, hoping to keep the questions to a minimum.

Kevin leaned to his left, over to a gray filing cabinet next to his desk. He pulled open a drawer and took out a yellow folder with the letters TPD stenciled on the cover. Kevin dropped it on his desk, opened it, and slowly started to flip through the pages.

"Here we go. We have their IDs and criminal history. The driver's name was Anthony Maisto, and the passenger was Vincent Cimilucca. Maisto was a known drug dealer from Brooklyn. He did five years in East Jersey State Prison for possession and distribution, and had a long rap sheet for car theft, and burglaries. Cimilucca was originally from Irvington and a smaller rap sheet that included several arrests for possession of cocaine. Nothing serious though, not much that would involve him with a big-time drug ring. Looks like the guy was just a small-time hood with a drug addiction."

Joey nodded as if he already knew the story. "What about the Jeep? Anything else on the registered owner?"

Kevin shrugged his shoulders and said, "We know it was leased by the Hilltop Corporation, but nothing further." He flipped through a few more pages and stopped for a moment as he glanced at another report before he finally looked up. "I'm reading this first responder report, and it's signed by you. I didn't realize you were the first one on scene."

"I was the first to arrive. One of the worst accidents I've seen in a long time." Joey said, starting to feel anxious inside.

"It also says here that you called the accident into headquarters before it was dispatched. You must have been close by when it happened."

"It happened in my district," Joey said as he shifted in his seat. "The road was deserted when I saw the Jeep smashed against that tree. Both passengers were dead when I arrived. I'm not sure what the time frame was between the crash and me calling it in."

"Too bad your partner got all the glory. You should have been right beside him at the channel 12 interview."

"That's okay, Tom found the coke. He deserved all the recognition," Joey said.

"I'm glad you feel that way. You know, there are a lot of ass kissers and cutthroats in this department who would do anything to get promoted or assigned to the bureau," Kevin said seriously.

"That's why I'm still in patrol driving a black and white," Joey said, satisfied that he wasn't known for sucking up to the brass.

Kevin looked up at Joey. "Yeah, the happiest years I've had on the department were when I was in patrol with you guys."

On that note, Joey had heard enough. He didn't need Kevin to start telling old war stories about the past. He didn't have the time or the desire. "Not to change the subject, but could you let me know if you find out anything else about the Jeep? There was a lot of coke found at the accident, and I'm interested to know if there might be others involved. Just want to be on the safe side."

"I wish I could, but that's not going to happen," Kevin said, closing the file almost too dramatically.

"Why not?" Joey asked, his voice sharpening.

"Because someone from the chief's office sent me a memo telling me to close the case and stop any further investigation," Kevin said, trying to stay objective.

"I guess they have their reasons," Joey said, controlling his temper as he stood to leave.

"Sorry, Joe. I wish I had more."

"One more thing, Kevin," Joey said, pointing to the eight-by-ten picture behind Kevin. "When was that taken?"

Kevin turned and looked up at the wall, following Joey's finger. "That one? Last year at the awards dinner. The big guy is Dominick Zarza, and the rest you already know."

"Oh, the big real estate developer. Looks like he's holding an award too. What did he get his for?"

Kevin thought for a moment before he answered. "He received a civilian award for helping our narcotics bureau solve a drug case, my department received a letter of recognition."

"When did that happen?"

"Beginning of last year. We were working close with the county strike force on a small network of drug dealers. They were working out of an old warehouse in Red Bank. I believe Zarza owned the building and tipped off the chief."

"They give awards to anyone these days," Joey said, shaking his head in disbelief.

"It was good publicity for the town and department."

"Well, thanks for all your help," Joey said, walking toward the door.

"No problem, Joe, wish I had more. If I hear of anything else, I'll let you know," Kevin said.

"Thanks again, Kev," Joey said, shutting the door behind him.

"What an asshole the chief is," Joey said to himself as he walked back down the hall, remembering a police call he'd gotten four years ago. He had been dispatched to a domestic call on the south side of Two River, next to the low-income projects. The dispatch said a woman called 911, screaming that her husband was trying to kill her with a baseball bat and that she'd locked herself in the bedroom. Dispatch tried to keep her on the phone, but the phone went dead after another scream and a loud crash. Tom Brougham was his backup, and they were both on scene within minutes.

As Joey and Tom entered the house, they heard screaming in the rear bedroom. The place was a mess, with a smashed lamp on the living room floor, an old wooden coffee table lying on its side, and a plate of spaghetti splattered on the floor. There were several blobs of tomato sauce on the already stained couch and several empty beer bottles strewn about. Joey ceased his observation when he heard the woman scream again.

"Please stop! Don't hit me anymore! I'll do what you want."

"Fuck you, bitch," a drunken voice yelled back.

Joey and Tom rushed inside the bedroom and found the woman on the floor, wedged in the corner. Her knees were bent up into her chest, her arms cradling her head. The phone by her side had obviously been ripped out of the wall. The woman's drunken husband stood over her, swaying side to side, holding a baseball bat in his right hand and waving it over her head. He was oblivious to the two police officers standing behind him. The guy stood about six feet tall and must have weighed close to three hundred pounds, and his food-stained undershirt struggled to cover a huge beer belly that jiggled past his belt. Joey drew his gun immediately and pointed it at the man.

"Police! Put the bat down!"

Tom had his Mace in his right hand and quickly checked the position of the PR-24 baton that hung from the left side of his gun belt. Time seemed to stand still as Joey realized he'd have only a split second to decide what to do if the husband chose to take a swing at his wife—use deadly force or rely on Tom's Mace. Luckily, the husband turned and saw both officers. His bloodshot eyes focused on Joey holding a mean-looking service weapon that was pointed right at his chest.

"Drop the bat, asshole!" Tom yelled again.

The drunk swayed as he made a quarter turn and threw the bat at Tom's feet. Then turning his attention back to his wife, who was sobbing through swollen black eyes, he said, "I'll get you for this, you bitch." Suddenly, he raised his right arm to hit her again.

Instantly, Tom jumped in between and sprayed the Mace in the man's eyes from less than a foot away. The drunk immediately sank to his knees, howling and trying feverishly to wipe the liquid from his eyes. Joey and Tom jumped on the man and tried to control his arms enough to get the handcuffs around his wrists, but the husband continued to swing his arms violently. He grabbed blindly at anything around him.

Once again, Tom reacted quickly, pulled out his baton, and swung it around fast and hard. He made certain not to hit Joey, his partner, and connected solidly on the husband's right forearm. Tom's adrenaline was running high, and he swung again, this time hitting him on top of the shoulder. The drunk was getting tired, but he was still flailing around his meaty arms. Joey was able to get one of the cuffs around his right hand, but had trouble with the left.

Tom took another swing. "Put your arms behind your back, you scumbag! Goddamn wife beater!" He'd aimed his PR-24 for the guy's left forearm, but struck him instead on the head as the drunk tried to pull free of Joey's grasp. The blow to the head knocked him out immediately and gave him a deep cut over his right eye. When he was finally down and still, Joey finished cuffing him. Joey informed headquarters to send two ambulances to his location. The wife beater, known to Joey and Tom as Chris O'Reilly, was transported by the first aid squad to Riverside Hospital to be treated. At the hospital, O'Reilly had to be guarded by Tom until he was medically released by the doctor. Once released, he was taken back to headquarters, fingerprinted, and photographed, and put in a temporary holding cell. Joey stayed at the scene with Mrs. O'Reilly, who suffered two black eyes and several other bruises to her body. She gave Joey a signed written statement as to the events that took place prior to his arrival. Joey took digital photographs of her visible wounds, and she was taken by the second ambulance to Monmouth County hospital for medical attention. She was advised that a detective would be in touch with her in a day or so for a formal statement. After everyone had left, Joey stayed at the residence and took pictures of the inside of the house and retrieved the bat as evidence.

After leaving the scene and returning to headquarters, Joey and Tom spent the next two hours typing out complaints and reports. Joey had telephoned the assistant prosecutor, who approved complaints against Mr. O'Reilly for aggravated assault, possession of a weapon, possession of a weapon for an unlawful purpose, and resisting arrest. Joey then called the judge who set bail at fifty thousand dollars, full, no 10 percent bond. Mr. O'Reilly was then taken to the county jail in Freehold Township to await his court hearing.

The couple had a long history of domestic violence where arrests were usually made and restraining orders were filed, only to be dropped a week later. However, this was the worst domestic fight reported to date. A few days later, while Joey and Tom were on patrol, Joey received a call on his cell phone from Ann, the chief's secretary, giving him the heads-up that the chief was going to call them in about their domestic arrest.

Ann had worked in the police department as a civilian for more than twenty years, starting in the records bureau, moving up to the secretary for the captain of detectives, and then finally being promoted to the upstairs sanctum of the chief's office ten years ago. In fact, she'd been at the department a couple of years longer than Joey. He met her early on when she needed help with a flat tire just a few blocks from headquarters, and they'd been friends since. Over the years, Ann had worked with four different chiefs, and over the occasional coffee or visit to the chief's ivory tower, she confided in Joey that for the first time in her tenure, she just could not stomach the man who presently occupied the chair beyond her office. Joey had always made it clear that he wouldn't divulge any of the privileged information he received from her, and in fact, Ann had been a staunch ally throughout his painful divorce. As always, Ann was correct. Two hours later, Joey and Tom were summoned to the chief's office.

Chief Reinus had been promoted to his position five years ago for kissing the Mayor's ass and sucking up to the local politicians. He tried hard to be included in the political circles involving city council members and the mayor, and there was never any question among the officers in the patrol division about the chief's ambitions or allegiance. They were politically motivated only to improve his position with the local politicians and create a positive image with the residents of Two River. It was rumored around headquarters that the chief was only using his current position as a stepping-stone to get into the political arena, possibly to run for county sheriff or mayor. He was called Reinus the Anus behind his back, and it was clear to everyone other than him that he'd forgotten where he'd come from. Somewhere along the road to becoming chief, he had switched from being a cop to a wannabee politician. Reinus the Anus appeared to live above his means. On a salary of a hundred thirty thousand a year, he drove a new Mercedes Benz, owned a big house in the upscale town of Navesink, and had another on Long Beach Island. He wore expensive suits and shoes that made him look even less like a cop and more like a businessman. It was rumored that when his wife's father died, he inherited a boatload of money because he bought the house in LBI right after the funeral. His abode, as he called it, was rumored to be worth two million dollars. But everyone in the police department knew that a week after a rumor started, it usually became fact.

As Joey and Tom waited outside the chief's office, Joey could not think of anything they had done wrong. The domestic arrest two days ago went as well as could be expected, but they knew the chief wasn't known to give pats on the back. He took all the credit when things went right, and directed the blame to his officers when mistakes were made. Ann stuck her head out of the chief's office and gestured them inside; the chief was ready to see them. She opened the door for Joey and Tom and then left the office. Joey and Tom walked in and sat in the two chairs that faced the man's desk. He knew they were waiting, but instead of acknowledging their presence, he was on the phone, gazing out the second-story window above Main Street and laughing to someone on the other end. After several long minutes, the chief finally hung up the phone and rotated in his chair to face both of them. The smile he'd worn for the caller had evaporated. Because the meeting had nothing to do with the chief's personal interest, he was very direct and to the point.

"Do you two remember the domestic you had two days ago involving Mr. O'Reilly?"

Joey and Tom nodded their heads in unison.

"Well, his lawyer paid me a visit yesterday, he is suing the police department, the city, and everybody else who was involved with your arrest. He states that you used excessive force and acted in a manner unbecoming of a police officer."

Joey and Tom looked at each other in disbelief. Joey turned to the chief and said, "Excessive force? That bastard was going to kill her. He had a bat and was going to smash her head with it!"

"And that's another thing," the chief said, cutting him off. "Where do you get off calling civilians names like scumbag and wife beater? You're supposed to act like a professional at all times. I checked the videotape and heard the name-calling."

The chief took a deep breath, and Joey and Tom knew there was more to come.

"Mr. O'Reilly is back in the hospital with thirty stitches in his head, and his doctors are checking X-rays of his skull for any internal problems. His lawyer is filing a ten million-dollar lawsuit, and both of you are listed as co-defendants. I'm the chief of this department, and I don't need officers like you giving this department a bad name. There will be an internal investigation to determine whether any disciplinary action should be taken against the both of you."

"Listen, Chief," Joey said, trying to control his anger, "we did everything by the book."

Joey couldn't help but think that three days ago, O'Reilly was an unemployed alcoholic who beat his wife every Friday night just to let out his frustrations. Now some hungry lawyer is putting dollar signs in front of his eyes. Within the next few months, this guy will have O'Reilly seeing a half dozen doctors, from psychologists to chiropractors, treating him for his physical and psychological discomfort. The treatments will have been carefully orchestrated by the attorney, and the doctors will document all O'Reilly's newfound mental and physical problems caused by the traumatic event that was brought about by two cops who beat him unjustly.

Joey knew it was useless to argue with the man. "Okay, Chief. If that's the way you want it, then we reserve the right to an attorney and a union representative before we say anything else."

"I suggest you contact them ASAP. We're done here."

Joey and Tom got up and left the office without saying another word.

Five days later, Detective White, who was assigned to investigate the domestic dispute, caught Joey and Tom in the hallway of headquarters and said.

"Hey, do you guys know that when Mrs. O'Reilly found out about the ten million-dollar lawsuit, she refused to give me a formal statement against her husband and denied she was assaulted? She refused to sign the complaints! Matter of fact, someone in the family court said that she'd dropped the restraining order. She wants him back home when he is released from the hospital. Can you believe that?"

"Figures," Joey said, "but we still have the voluntary statement that she wrote and signed. Plus, we have the photos of her injuries."

"Yeah," said White, "but you know how it looks when the couple comes into court holding hands like they just came home from their honeymoon. She'll probably tell the judge that she fell or accidentally hit herself in both eyes with a doorknob."

"That's the thanks we get for saving her life," Tom said. "We'll be back there when the asshole gets drunk again. They always call when they need us, but could care less when everything is good. This job really sucks sometimes."

"That's the nature of the beast!" White said. "See you in the trenches, guys."

The lawsuit lingered for five stressful months but never made it to trial. The city settled out of court for two hundred thousand dollars, knowing it would cost them more money in attorney fees with a lengthy trial. The criminal charges were dropped against Joey and Tom just as fast as they were filed once settlement was made. The city also agreed–against the recommendations of Joey and Tom–to drop the charges against Mr. O'Reilly. O'Reilly's lawyer, Marc Schwarstein, who was well-known as an ambulance chaser, made a quick sixty-seven thousand while Mr. O'Reilly netted a hundred fourteen thousand minus twenty thousand in doctor fees for beating his wife.

Reinus the Anus suspended Joey and Tom for three days for actions unbecoming of a police officer, and he made sure that news of the suspensions were leaked to the media so that the public would be aware that he was doing everything he could to make certain that his officers remained respectful to the residents of Two River.

Joey walked to his car outside of headquarters and finally noticed his throbbing headache. He reached for his cell phone, found Ann at the beginning of his contacts, and pressed Send. She answered after the third ring.

"Ann, this is Joey. How's it going?"

"Good, Joey. Is everything all right?"

"I think so, but I was wondering why the chief called Tommy into his office the other day asking questions about the accident. You know how he is. Nothing good usually comes out of those meetings." Joey tried his best not to sound overly concerned.

The silence on the other end persisted for several seconds, and Joey thought they had gotten disconnected. "Are you there, Ann?"

"I'm here Joe. I'm just not sure why the chief called him in. He has been very tight-lipped lately. If I find out, I'll give you a call," Ann said.

"Thanks, Ann."

"No problem, Joe."

Thank God for cell phones, Joey thought. Every phone line in headquarters is tapped.

Chapter 9

T HE JEEP'S REGISTERED owner was the Hilltop Corporation, which had a PO Box address in Red Bank. Joey knew that Hilltop was a subsidiary of a company owned by Nordella Group Enterprises, the biggest construction and land development company on the East Coast.

Joey searched Google using the Nordella Group as the topic, and within seconds, he was looking at tens of thousands of articles on the company that spanned a fifty-year period. The articles revealed that Nordella's main offices were located in Freehold, and the company was owned by Dominick Zarza. The Nordella Group was responsible for building and developing the most expensive properties in Monmouth County. It had made headlines in the late sixties when it built and sold the first million-dollar homes in Rumson before spreading out to other affluent towns, such as Holmdel and Colts Neck. It was also the developer of the most expensive waterfront properties in New Jersey, which stretched from Perth Amboy down to Cape May.

Dominick's father, Raffio, started the business in Monmouth County during the late fifties and expanded steadily throughout the state and eventually all the way south to Florida in the seventies and eighties. Nowadays, the company had offices in the Carolinas and Florida.

Raffio was a savvy businessman who knew the value of real estate. He believed that the only way to acquire great wealth was through real estate, and he made it his life's ambition to acquire as much of both as he could. Not only did Raffio develop and build million-dollar estate homes, but he also built huge apartment buildings, commercial properties, and strip malls. He usually kept the most valuable real estate for himself for which he charged premium rent. Over time, Raffio gathered so much rental property that he started two other companies, Hilltop and Nordella Investments. Hilltop was responsible for the maintenance and upkeep of the properties while Nordella Investments was the management arm that handled the monthly rents, evictions, and vacant space management when it became available.

Raffio was an old-school Italian businessman who did not like politics and did not trust politicians, and although he was always invited to the big political functions given by state senators or the governor, he never went. The only invitation he ever accepted was from President Gerald Ford in 1976 during which he received a humanitarian award at the White House. In contrast, he was honored to have met Jesse Owens and witnessed him receive the Presidential Medal of Freedom, the highest award bestowed upon a civilian in recognition of his winning four gold medals during the 1936 Olympics. It was at these Olympic Games that made Adolf Hitler walk out of the stadium, enraged that a black man could defeat his superior white race. The other political functions were usually held simply to seek donations. At one time, Raffio was invited to a fund-raiser for Vice President Gore. It was sponsored by Jon Bon Jovi at his multimillion-dollar mansion on the Navesink River, but Raffio declined and instead sent his son, Dominick. Raffio knew that making money was difficult, but he also realized keeping it was even harder. The Nordella Group and its subsidiaries were one of the few privately owned companies that were worth over a billion dollars.

Joey read as many articles as he could find on the Nordella Group. After hours of research on the computer, Joey was satisfied that Dominick was not behind the drug deal.

Chapter 10

IT WAS THE first day on night shift for Joey and Tom, both of whom were on patrol in their separate police cars. It was Joey's idea to meet in the Starbucks parking lot. Joey arrived first and bought two large iced coffees as he waited. Tom drove up a few minutes later. They parked their patrol cars at the rear of the lot and opposite each other so that their driver's side windows were just inches away. With their windows opened and the air conditioners running full blast, Joey reached out and handed Tom his drink. It was a hot and humid night, and Joey could feel the sweat rolling down his back underneath his bulletproof vest. It was the tenth of August, six days after the accident, and just sixty minutes remained before the meeting with the black Blazer at Harbor Park.

Joey looked across to Tom as he finished a hearty drink. "Hopefully, no one will be there tonight. If it's just an asshole busting your balls, he might be in the park, hanging around to see if you show up just to get a good laugh. So keep an eye out for anybody who might be in the area."

Tom sipped at his coffee and said, "I can't believe this is really happening, being harassed and threatened by a drug dealer or some other asshole." Tom paused, looking straight ahead and continued, "Whoever called my house better not show up tonight. If I catch him, he'll find himself in jail with my foot up his ass."

"Tom, we have an advantage," Joey said. "No matter who's out there, they won't be expecting you to show up on duty in your patrol car. We'll check out anyone we see at the park–get their IDs and run them for warrants–and if they give us any shit, we'll lock 'em up."

"What if the black Blazer is there waiting for me?" Tom asked.

"Listen, I'll drive through the park first and see if it's there. If I see it, I'll stop and check out the driver–treat it like a suspicious vehicle. They'll think I'm just another cop patrolling the park. I'll put their names over the radio and let headquarters check for warrants. If you recognize a name, you can back me up and put your foot up his ass."

"What about the mobile video camera and mic?" Tom asked.

"You leave yours on. I'll shut mine off. I don't need the chief checking the video and suspending me for calling the driver an asshole."

Tom made it clear that he didn't like the idea. "You know the chief has an administrative order that the camera and mic are on at all times while we're on the job, especially on traffic stops. He suspended Rengifo for two days because he didn't have his camera on when he pulled over that black woman, the one who signed a complaint against him for making racial remarks. It was her word against his, and the department sided with her. He couldn't prove a thing since nothing was on tape."

"I think it would be better if I shut mine off. I'll write a report that my camera had a malfunction and wouldn't record," Joey said, disregarding the chief's order.

"I guess," Tom said, sipping more of his coffee.

Joey could see that his partner wasn't sold on the idea, but his mind was set.

∧ ∧ ∧ ∧ ∧ ∧ ∧

Harbor Park was a small public reserve that extended from River Road and sloped down a hill to the Navesink River. The only way to get into the park by car was by taking Wharf Avenue from River Road, but the route led to a small hill in a rectangular parking lot that faced the water. At the far end was a playground and two tennis courts, both of which closed at dusk. Between the parking lot and river, a boardwalk ran the length of the park with a small pier that jetted out some twenty feet into the water. During the day, the park was busy with moms walking their kids in strollers, letting them loose in the playground. At lunchtime, the benches were always full of businessmen and women, and the local fishermen had their particular spots on the pier, holding their poles over the side and waiting for a nibble. Near the entrance stood a large sign that cautioned anyone who cared to read it, "Park Closed After Sundown." There was a city ordinance in effect that prohibited people from being in the park during the hours of darkness, and it was occasionally enforced by the police. The city council ratified the new ordinance so that the police could legally chase out juveniles who congregated there after hours to drink alcohol and do drugs. The ordinance obviously worked since the park had been very quiet over the summer with no noise complaints from owners of the huge mansions across the Navesink River.

∧ ∧ ∧ ∧ ∧ ∧ ∧

A little after ten o'clock, the black Blazer turned onto Wharf Avenue and drove past the big sign in the park. The Blazer drove to the end of the parking lot and backed into the last space, away from the light being spat out by the moth-riddled overhead lamppost. Michael Power was driving, and Carlos Ferrer was sitting shotgun. Michael had no specific plan, he just wanted to get the money from the dirty cop and get the hell out of there. Power hated dealing with cops. Since he was a kid, he'd been in trouble with the police. By the time he was eighteen years old, he had a rap sheet a mile long, largely because of a temper he couldn't control. When he was seven, Michael was arrested for shoplifting, and then at nine, he was busted for burglary. He stole his first car at thirteen and received three years in a juvenile detention center, where he learned how to fight and use a knife. He stood trial as an adult when he was seventeen for stabbing his father to death, but he was acquitted by the judge due to a legal technicality for which the prosecution was responsible. Then when he was twenty-two, his life took another twist. Michael was involved with a drug deal that went very bad. An argument ensued, guns were drawn, and shots were fired. Michael was shot in the leg, but he killed the two Columbians who were on the other side of the deal. Unknown to Michael, one of the Columbians that he killed also ripped off Dominick in an unrelated transaction. Dominick had a $50,000 contract put on the Columbian's head, and as fate would have it, Dominick gave Michael $50,000 and a job he couldn't refuse. Michael felt good about working for Dominick. He had protection and was under the umbrella of Dominick's empire. He was glad to be with a family and off the streets grinding out dangerous drug deals with street gangs.

Michael picked Carlos to come with him not because of his intelligence, but because he was the biggest meanest-looking person he had ever known. Carlos could simply look at someone and make the person shit his–or her–pants. Literally. He didn't need to say a word. Michael glanced over at Carlos who was staring out the window. He had a barrel chest, and Michael could see the bulge of the gun shoved inside the shoulder holster underneath his jacket. Michael advised Carlos not to talk; he would handle everything.

Chapter 11

IT ALL STARTED when Dominick met a guy named Mark Keats in a plush New York nightclub. Dominick was sitting at the bar, having a beer and watching a man who looked to be ten years younger than he was. The guy was ordering five hundred-dollar bottles of Champagne and handing out full glasses to the crowd gathered around him. It appeared as though he had a substantial amount of money as well as a great personality. He was good-looking and seemed to have the attention of all the ladies in the room. The younger man was surrounded by a large group of people, and everyone was leaving the dance floor to migrate toward him. When everyone was standing around him, he held his glass aloft and announced, "To CVIM." Everybody cheered and clapped, and it looked as though most of the people knew him. Soon enough, the clapping stopped, and the crowd thinned out as the well-wishers headed back to the dance floor—except for most of the women. They continued to stand around him, smiling and posing like models.

The scene reminded Dominick of *The Bachelor* show on TV. Dominick ordered another beer and laughed to himself as he thought about the situation. *Look at this guy, I could buy and sell him. If they only knew I was mentioned in GQ as one of the most desirable bachelors in the country.* Dominick was feeling a little left out; after all, he was a Zarza, the only Zarza, and one of the wealthiest people in the country. *The women are hanging around that guy just because he throws around a few thousand dollars.* Dominick gestured to Yancy, the bartender, who had a polished bald head and the longest handlebar mustache that he had ever seen.

"What can I get you, Mr. Zarza?"

"Do you know who that guy is?" asked Dominick.

"That's Mark Keats, a very successful stockbroker. I believe he's celebrating a huge deal he just completed."

"Buy him another bottle and put it on my tab."

"No problem, Mr. Zarza," said the bartender. He darted away for a moment only to return in a flash with another bottle of champagne, which he opened in front of Mark, nodding in Dominick's direction.

Mark lifted his glass toward Dominick and took a sip before he turned his attention back to his attentive audience saying something funny. The girls all laughed in unison. Mark patted the pretty brunette on her rear end and left his admirers standing in a small group. He walked a few seats down to where Dominick was sitting.

"Thanks for the drink, but I should be the one who's buying."

"What for?" asked Dominick.

"For having good fortune, for being an integral part of capitalism, which makes this the best place in the world. It is utterly fantastic to live in a country where great fortunes can be made or lost in an instant. Sorry, I don't mean to carry on. I'm Mark Keats." He stuck out a hand.

"Dominick Zarza," he said with an expectant smile. He was waiting for a reaction from Keats but never got one. It was apparent that Mark didn't know who he was.

Mark had a magnetic personality, and they hit it off from the start. Mark explained to Dominick how he traded stocks and bonds and had just finished a takeover that netted his firm a hundred million dollars. Mark owned his own firm, Stenson Investments, and only worked with the CEOs of *Fortune* 500 companies. Most of his deals were worth millions despite the fact that the market was on a downward curve. But Mark was the best there was at what he did and made money regardless of the condition of the market.

Dominick listened and was impressed by the amount of money that could be made in the stock market, all without the hassle of actually owning anything. No collecting of rent, no lawn maintenance or property managers, and no eviction notices. Just buying and selling the right stock. Dominick was feeling more comfortable with Mark, and the beers were starting to give him a buzz.

"You don't know who I am, do you?"

"Should I? You said you were in real estate. Were we ever involved in a stock deal?"

"No, I never bought a stock in my life. But I do happen to own a lot of real estate. I'm the owner of the Nordella Group."

Mark's eyebrow's rose instinctively. "I'm very impressed. I've read many articles about your company in the investment journals. My apologies for not putting the name Zarza with the company," he said.

"Don't apologize. My father did it on purpose. He named the company after a small town in Italy where he was born. He wanted to be left alone when he was out in public, and for a while, people never associated the Zarza name with the Nordella Group. But after the company grew and my father's picture was on the cover of most of the investment magazines, his anonymity was over."

"I remember reading articles about your father in the *Wall Street Journal*, how he started from scratch and built the biggest real estate company in the country. Your father was considered a legend. You must be very proud of him," Mark said, taking a sip of his champagne.

Dominick felt the anxiety build in his throat as Mark praised his father. He knew that the feeling of insecurity would follow soon after. Thoughts of his father and his childhood started to flash back. His father, Raffio, was considered a great businessman by his peers and was often referred to as the Godfather of real estate. He spent many hours at the office, and many weekends traveling to different construction sites along the coast. He was never home, and Dominick spent most of his time with his mother, Carmela, whom he loved and cherished. Carmela spoiled her only son, but she was also the one who threw Dominick his first baseball and cheered him when he got his first base hit. On Father's Day, Dominick would joke with his mother and give her the Father's Day card that he'd bought, saying that she deserved it more than his dad. When Raffio would finally come home, he wound up spending most of his time in his study talking business in long-distance phone calls. For Raffio, making great wealth was his priority, and for that, his family paid the price.

Dominick's mother died of breast cancer when he was fourteen. This had deeply devastated Dominick, and over the next several years, he had become withdrawn and unwilling to leave the house. He simply stayed home and watched gangster movies. *The Godfather* was his favorite. After his mother's death, Raffio gave Dominick anything he wanted, anytime he wanted it. Dominick knew that his father didn't want him to have any more painful life experiences, so he shielded him as much as he could from the realities of life. Because of that, Dominick never learned his father's work ethic or the value of a dollar.

Dominick cursed his father and blamed him for his mother's death. From the day his mother died, Dominick held a grudge against his father for not being there when they needed him.

As the only child, when Raffio died, Dominick inherited a billion-dollar business at the age of thirty-nine. The first thing on Dominick's agenda was to sell his father's five million-dollar house and buy the biggest most expensive place in Monmouth County. It wasn't long before he found a veritable fortress in the township of Rumson, high on a hilltop overlooking the Shrewsbury River and Atlantic Ocean. It was situated on ten acres of the most sought-after property. The estate came with a tennis court and two inground heated pools, one outside and one inside. A smaller adjacent house was used for the maids and servants quarters, and the entire package cost a meager twenty million dollars.

Dominick finally felt free to do what he pleased and no longer had to live in his father's shadow. He wanted to make his own mark in life and wanted to be respected for his accomplishments rather than those of his father.

"Hey, you still with me?" Mark asked waving his glass in front of Dominick's face.

"Oh . . . Sorry . . . You're right. My father was a helluva businessman." Dominick pushed out the words as he stood up.

"Where you going? The night's still young." Mark said with his contagious smile, and then turned his head toward the attractive brunette who was staring at him a few seats away.

"Going to the men's room. Beer makes me piss every ten minutes."

Mark let out a genuine laugh. "You should be drinking Champagne!–Listen, when you get back, come join us. Drinks are on me, I insist."

Dominick gave Mark a forced smile, nodded his head as he walked away. He needed a couple minutes alone.

Despite the difference in their business dealings and upbringing, Dominick and Mark became friends. They became acquaintances and went out twice a week together to the most vogue nightspots, at times engaging in a competition to determine who could spend the most money. It was a new approach to life for Dominick, and Mark was showing him how to enjoy every day of it. Mark introduced him to his stable of pretty women and turned him onto a drug called cocaine. Mark explained to Dominick how women are addicted to coke and will do anything for it.

As the friendship grew, Dominick spent more time away from the business and made himself available anytime Mark wanted to go out. As Dominick's drug habit increased, so did his taste for women and the finer things in life. Dominick's newest toy was a Gulfstream, the best personal jet money could buy for which he paid a cool forty-five million. The jet was equipped with two large bedrooms, each with its own bathroom, and an office with enough technology to run his business from six miles above the Earth. He employed two pilots who were on call 24/7, paying them an extra two hundred thousand a year. The hangar and maintenance fees amounted to another seventy thousand a year. Dominick never thought twice after a night of partying to round up a couple of women at three in the morning and fly to the Bahamas for breakfast. For an average-looking guy who was noticeably overweight, Dominick was beginning to believe he too had a way with the women.

As time went by, Dominick saw less and less of Mark. Mark had told him on several occasions that he was busy on another deal and was working twelve-hour days, six days a week. Mark never told Dominick anything specific about the deal, but insinuated that it was huge. *Another fortune to be made by Stenson Investments,* Dominick thought. He then considered his own company, the Nordella Group, which had endured the rise and fall of the real estate market over a fifty-year period. Real estate went flat in the eighties but then spiraled up and eventually doubled in value during the nineties–just to go flat again when the stock market hit new turbulence caused by the technology boom and all the start-up dot-coms. During the early nineties, more people were becoming millionaires than ever before. The stock market was setting new high records, and trillions of dollars were pouring into mutual funds. Everyone in the market was making money, and based on the rate of return promised by mutual funds, most middle managers in America were planning early retirements.

As Dominick watched the stock market soar, he felt left out. All of his money was in real estate, which had fallen out of favor. He wanted to make a move into the market but held back, only to be surprised when the bubble busted, leaving most people holding stocks and mutual funds that were worthless. Dominick patted himself on the back for making the right decision, and he knew his time would come eventually. As the nineties ended, real estate came back with a vengeance, doubling in value, and Dominick's empire benefitted tremendously from the positive cycle. Dominick never thought he would find the investment opportunity he had wanted, one that would give him his own mark in history and would distinguish him as a stock market genius. He would become his own man, thus shutting up those who talked about him behind his back and derided the spoiled rich kid for spending all of his daddy's money. When he went to political dinners, he would certainly get the respect he deserved.

∧ ∧ ∧ ∧ ∧ ∧ ∧

It was on a Sunday that Dominick finally managed to get Mark away from the office. Dominick had his limo collect Mark at his New York brownstone on East 59th Street by Madison Avenue and take him to Monmouth Executive Airport in Farmingdale, where the wealthiest people kept their personal jets. Dominick wanted to show off his new toy to Mark and had planned a two-day trip to Las Vegas. The Palms Casino had comped Dominick the top penthouse suite for as long as he wanted to stay, along with anything he needed. He had the highest casino rating possible and was referred to as a member of the M&M club. In Las Vegas, that meant you could afford to lose a million a minute. To have such a high roller with a growing reputation for squandering his daddy's fortune, the casino would allow Dominick to do whatever he wanted and would spare no effort–or expense–to make his stay as comfortable as possible. That usually meant giving Dominick a five thousand-square-foot suite that came with a grand piano, a heated pool, a personal chef and bartender, and a blackjack table–complete with a dealer.

Mark arrived at Monmouth Executive Airport and was greeted by Dominick with a handshake as he exited the black stretch limo and was led to the stairs of the Gulfstream. As they approached the steps, Mark lagged behind and called to Dominick as he was about to climb the steps, "Dom, listen. I'm sorry, but I can't do two days in Vegas. I have a lot of work to do, and I don't need anything clouding my mind."

Dominick turned and looked at Mark's face. It was void of his usual upbeat energy. He looked stressed, a trait that Dominick was not used to.

"You do look a little tired. I have a better idea than Vegas. C'mon, follow me. You won't be disappointed." Dominick said, climbing the steps.

Mark shrugged and followed up the steps until they were greeted by a very pretty young attendant, waiting for them at the cabin door. The inside of the cabin was furnished with the finest quality leather chairs and couches and was decorated with highly polished mahogany. There was another young woman in a short skirt standing at the bar, waiting to take their drink orders. Mark immediately sunk into one of the leather couches and said, "I could fall right to sleep. I haven't realized how hard I've been working lately, but to be honest, I'm still behind schedule and need to put in longer hours."

Dominick sat down in a huge leather recliner across from Mark and picked up the phone that was attached to the cabin wall that connected him directly to the pilot and said, "Change of plans, Dan. We're going to South Beach. Call ahead and let them know we're coming to dinner." Dominick hung up and turned toward Mark who looked a little confused.

"South Beach?"

Dominick nodded. "The Nordella Group owns the Melia Caribe hotel in South Beach. It has one of the best restaurants in town. I'll have you home by midnight."

Mark smiled, showing his approval.

Dominick motioned to the cute stewardess to bring out a bottle of his favorite wine with two glasses. Moments later, she was back with their drinks and disappeared somewhere in the front cabin. Dominick figured he would let Mark relax a bit before he gave him the tour of his new toy.

The takeoff went very smoothly, and the two men sat for several minutes looking out the window over Monmouth County as the homes became smaller. Eventually, the landscape turned into neat green squares separated by tiny roads with cars that looked like little Matchbox toys.

"Mark, you seem to be working much too hard these days," Dominick said. "You need to slow down."

"I wish I could, but I enjoy it too much. I love putting deals together and merging companies. It's challenging and hard work, but that's what makes it fun. Capitalism at its finest, man."

Mark seemed to have gotten a jolt of energy from the explanation, and Dominick noticed that he sat up straight. It was clear that the guy loved his work. Dominick offered Mark a line of coke, but Mark refused.

"C'mon, Mark. I bought it off your contact, it's great stuff," he said, leaning over and snorting a line in each nostril.

"Nope. When I'm working, I give up drugs and wild women. I give everything I've got to my clients. They pay me well, and they deserve my best."

"Wow," said Dominick, "I need more people like you working for me!"

"You couldn't afford me," Mark said, laughing. Then he glanced around the interior of the Gulfstream and said, "Then again, I could be wrong—which seldom happens."

"If you're never wrong, then maybe I should be involved in this big deal that you're so busy with. I could use a change. I've been involved with real estate all my life, maybe it would be exciting to get into the stock market."

"Hmmm, I never figured you as being a player in one of my deals. I thought you were happy just jet-setting around the world while your real estate increased in value. But if you're serious, I mean really serious, I believe Stenson Investments can take the Nordella Group to a new financial high with the help of *Wall Street.*

"I'm listening," Dominick said. The feelings of inferiority he normally had around Mark dissipated, thanks in large part to the cocaine. It was always great for his self-esteem and confidence. For the first time since his father had died, Dominick felt like a businessman. It was he who met Mark, and it was Dominick who was going to be responsible for taking Nordella to a new level. Dominick was proud of himself; he was going to make billions, which was more than he could say for his father.

"First of all, if you want to talk business, there will be no more drugs or booze. I don't want to be misunderstood, and I don't want you to be influenced by anything other than good old common sense. So if that's all right with you, I'll tell you the specifics over dinner."

Dominick lifted his wineglass toward Mark and said, "This is my last drink."

The flight took a little over ninety minutes, and the limo was waiting for Dominick and Mark on the tarmac as the Gulfstream taxied down the runway and came to a stop. The management at the Melia Caribe had been notified that Mr. Zarza would be having dinner in the elegant Carmela Room, named after his mother, which was a four-star restaurant and one of the finest in Miami.

The car deposited Dominick and Mark at the hotel, and as expected, they were given the red-carpet treatment. They were seated at Dominick's favorite table by the window overlooking the ocean and South Beach. No menus were brought to the table. Every time Dominick visited the restaurant with friends, he instructed the head chef to create a dinner that would impress his guest, and the chef never disappointed him. The only information the chef required was the guest's preference of cuisine. With a salary of over 250k a year, Dominick had complete confidence in him.

The service and presentation of food were exceptional. Dominick's confidence was building, and through the cocaine and the excitement of the business deal, he had lost his appetite and was in no rush to eat. Most of the first three courses that were served went untouched by Dominick, but Mark appeared to be enjoying every bit of the meal. Finally, Mark lifted his head and said, "This is one of the best meals I have ever eaten!"

"They're just the appetizers. Wait till the main course."

"This is delicious," Mark said, swallowing a small piece of an unknown fish.

As Mark continued to enjoy his meal, Dominick's curiosity grew by the second. He sat there and played with his food and had not eaten a morsel. When Mark had finished, the waiters had come out from nowhere and cleared off the table, filled the water glasses with Perrier, and refolded their napkins. When the waiters retreated back into the shadows, Mark started the conversation in a whisper, looking around as if to make sure nobody was within earshot to hear what he was about to say. Mark wiped his mouth with the napkin and leaned closer to Dominick.

"I know of a small biotech company." Mark stopped talking and looked around again before he continued. "The company has just completed a stage 2 trial for a drug called Zybris. This drug is supposed to stop and, in most cases, cure prostate cancer. It is going to be the biggest breakthrough in medical history in fighting cancer."

Mark stopped talking so that Dominick could digest the importance of what he had just said. Dominick stared at Mark, not missing a word he was saying. Two waiters approached the table and placed two huge steaming hot plates in front of them. Dominick gave them an impatient wave of his hand, adding, "Don't bother us! Can't you see we're busy?"

The one waiter stopped and bowed his head slightly. "Yes, Mr. Zarza. Sorry." And both walked away cursing the owner under their breath.

Mark continued in a low whisper, "The company is getting ready for the third and final stage of testing, making sure there are no fatal side effects to the drug. The drug must be as effective as possible since it's on the fast track for approval by the FDA."

Mark paused again to make sure Dominick was following. "The company is called Delta Services Incorporated and trades under the symbol DSSI on the NASDAQ. The company is very well managed, but it's running low on financing. They have spent more than a billion dollars in research and development to get the drug to this point, but they're concerned that one of the giant pharmaceutical companies with a lot of cash will buy them out and take over DSSI's management. Of course, that would mean that the new owner would get all the credit—and all the profits. DSSI needs to hold out until it completes phase 3, and then Zybris will be worth tens of billions. At that point, the big drug companies will be drooling to get a piece of the action, and they'll be willing to pay big money for it."

Mark definitely had Dominick's attention. Neither one had touched the food, and none of the waiters dared to clear away the table while Mr. Zarza's guest was still speaking.

"I have four investors on board as we speak, but I need a fifth to complete the deal. But I have already said too much, and if you're not interested, I need to know now. If the other investors knew what I was telling you before you committed, I would be jeopardizing the deal."

Dominick had a tough time controlling his eagerness and did not want to appear too enthusiastic. "I like what you said so far, but how do you know all this? And who are the other four investors?"

Mark was surprised that Dominick's first question was not what the other four had asked first, which was, *how much will it cost?* He was well prepared with all the answers. "It is my business to know, Dominick, that's what I get paid for. It is information that only comes along once in a lifetime, and I just happened to be at the right place at the right time. I can't divulge my source for this information, but if you are coming on board as the fifth investor, I can give you the names of the others. I'm sure you will recognize their names, they were also listed in the *Forbes* 100 most wealthiest."

Dominick desperately felt the need for another hit of coke and excused himself to the bathroom. Several minutes later, he returned looking and feeling energized. "Count me in."

Mark nodded almost imperceptibly. His hand gripped the napkin under the table so tight, that it went numb. His eyes came to life, but his voice stayed even.

"Here's the deal. Each investor will put up two hundred million, a total of a billion dollars—less my 10 percent commission, of course—for 60 percent of DSSI. All of you will agree not to interfere with management. The money will be more than enough to get Zybris through the third trial period and on the market for distribution. Your investment should give you a return of more than 400 percent in less than two years!"

Dominick's head was spinning as he tried to comprehend the profit he would make in such a short time. It took his father fifty years to make a billion, but he would be able to make the same in less than two. Visions of dollar signs clouded Dominick's cocaine-infused mind, and he came up with an idea that even surprised Mark.

"Mark, why don't I finance the whole deal? We'll forget about the other four. I could talk to my accountant. I'm sure I could come up with a billion dollars even if I have to leverage some properties."

Mark's eyebrows rose involuntarily. A quick grin that started to form quickly vanished from the corners of his mouth. "It wouldn't be good business to cut out the other four. I mean, I've done deals with them before. I don't like to burn my bridges."

"But wouldn't it be better to deal with just me? One person, instead of five?"

Mark nodded his head very slowly as if he was in deep thought and said, "I do agree on that. It would be easier with just you."

"Listen. Since there's billions to be made, I'll give you 20 percent commission. Just drop the other four. It'll be more for us."

A huge smile slowly crept across Mark's face as he said, "It would be a pleasure working with you, Dom. For an extra hundred mil, I could afford to lose the other four as clients. They're egotistical assholes anyway."

The two sealed the deal with a handshake, and all the legalities would be taken care of by the attorneys. Dominick ordered a thousand-dollar bottle of champagne to celebrate a day he would never forget.

Chapter 12

J OEY SAW THE vehicle turn onto Wharf Street. The windows of the black Chevy Blazer were tinted, so he could not see the driver or identify how many occupants were inside. He waited a few minutes before he drove toward the park and down the hill. As the law required, the park appeared totally deserted except for the Blazer at the end of the parking lot. Tom was in his patrol car that was parked on River Road above the park, two very short blocks away. Joey cruised slowly down the hill, and as he got closer, he saw through the front windshield that there were at least two occupants in the front seats. He spotted the New Jersey plate and plugged the number HJK27B into his laptop computer. In a matter of seconds, the Blazer's registered owner popped up on the LCD monitor, and it took Joey by surprise. Once again, it was listed as the Hilltop Corporation, with an address in Red Bank. He knew that the Hilltop was a landscaping company owned by the infamous Nordella Group from Two River, of which Dominick Zarza was the owner. In fact, it was he who'd put Two River on the map. A million questions popped into Joey's mind. *Who are these guys? Are they involved with the drugs from the Jeep? Does the money belong to them? Are they connected to the Nordella Group? Does Zarza know what his employees are involved with–?* Joey remembered seeing the picture of Reinus the Anus standing beside the mayor, who was accepting a check from Zarza. The chief probably had a hundred copies made and hung one on every wall of his house, he thought.

Shifting back to the Blazer, Joey realized that he did not like the position of his patrol car. He would have preferred to be behind the two guys and approach the driver's side window from the rear, but the driver had taken that into consideration when he backed the vehicle into the parking space. Settling for the hand he'd been dealt, Joey stopped his patrol car perpendicular to the front of the Blazer. He shut off his mobile video camera and microphone and got out. Joey walked around the rear of his car and stopped at the driver's side window of the Blazer. The dark-tinted window slid down almost immediately.

"Can I see your license, registration, and insurance card, please?"

Michael stared up at the officer, knowing he was not the one who had been on channel 12 news. He confirmed that quickly by reading the nameplate just below his badge: PO Sabba. "No problem, Officer," he said, reaching inside a coat pocket, searching for the wallet he kept just above his 9 mm. "What did we do wrong?"

"The park closes at dusk, you're not supposed to be here," Joey said, trying hard to recognize the driver.

"Didn't know that," Michael said, handing Joey his credentials.

"You do now. What about your friend, does he have ID?"

Carlos looked toward the open window from the passenger seat as Joey bent lower to get a better look. He'd seen some bad-looking dudes in his career, but this guy would make Freddy Krueger run the other way. Joey tried to hide his reaction, but it was too late; Michael had already picked up on it.

Michael said, "This is my friend Carlos, and I don't think he really wants or needs to show you any ID, Officer."

Tom slowly drove toward Wharf Avenue and had his cruiser hidden behind a group of bushes nearby. He could see Joey speaking with the driver of the Blazer, but he couldn't make out what was being said.

Joey knew from experience that these guys were not intimidated by a blue uniform and a badge, and they could care less what he had to say. Joey knew what they wanted–*his* money. He glanced at the name on the driver's license, Michael Power.

"Michael, we can do this the easy way or the hard way. In either case, I'm going to get that fat fuck's ID."

As Joey finished speaking, Carlos's right hand moved closer to the bulge in his jacket, but Michael motioned for him to stop.

Joey was convinced that these two guys were in business for themselves, using a company car, trying to make a quick buck dealing cocaine. They looked and sounded like street thugs, the ones the narcs busted every other week. He decided right then that no connection existed between these two thugs and any New York or New Jersey crime family, and the conclusion gave him an immediate sigh of relief.

"Why don't we both stop with the bullshit, Sabba. Where's your partner in crime, Tom Brougham? He was supposed to meet us here, not you," Michael spat.

"He's not coming, and he doesn't have anything for you. I know why you're here and what you want." Joey paused and allowed a thin smile to cross his face. He followed with a stone-cold look that pierced Michael's bravado. "But guess what, asshole, you're not going to get it. Consider yourselves lucky I don't throw your asses in jail. You hear what I'm saying?"

Michael's eyes glistened; their oily blackness made him appear crazed. He certainly wasn't intimidated; instead, he was angry. Dominick had made it clear that Michael could not come back empty-handed.

"Don't threaten me, man. You are the same as us, you just have a badge. You don't know who you're fucking with here, Sabba. Trust me, it would be best to just give me the money. That way, nobody needs to get hurt. After that, you can go back playing cops and robbers with the local yokels."

Michael was getting braver just hearing himself speak. He felt himself taking control of the situation and decided to press on. "Look, we know where you and Brougham live and what kind of cars you drive. It sure would be a shame if anything happened to Brougham's wife or his kids, or if your boat somehow blew up while you were out sailing around Sandy Hook." He knew he'd said too much, but he wasn't too concerned. After all, Officer Sabba was as good as dead.

Joey's mind was racing as he struggled to stay focused. He was thoroughly confused by how this thug knew so much about him and his partner. "You are full of shit, and your threats will wind up putting you in jail for a long time, asshole. Anyone with a computer could get that information."

Instead of being cowed by Joey's demeanor, Michael's attitude became even cockier. "You're the asshole. I know everything about you and Brougham, and it didn't take a computer to find it. The only thing we didn't know was who took the money. It wasn't Brougham at all, it was—"

Joey cut him off. "You want your money? I'll give it to you." Joey spun away, walked back to his vehicle, and opened the trunk.

"After we get the money, shoot him," Michael said. Carlos nodded and smiled.

Joey reached into the trunk and pulled out a white brick of cocaine. He held it in his right hand alongside his leg as he returned to the Blazer and pitched the kilo through the driver's side window as hard as he could. "Here's all the money you're going to get."

The kilo smashed against the center console and burst open. The white powder exploded all over Carlos in the passenger seat, making it appear as though he'd been coated in flour.

"Now you're both under arrest for the possession of a controlled dangerous substance."

Michael had all he could take. He'd killed people for less, but he was determined to control his temper so that he could get Dominick's money. But Michael did not anticipate Carlos doing something stupid. Despite being covered in white powder, Carlos pulled his gun, pointed it at the driver's side window, and pulled the trigger. Inside the car, the shot was deafening, and it caught Michael by complete surprise.

The slug hit Joey in the left shoulder and spun him back, but his actions were fast and deadly. He drew his weapon and fired five rounds into the Blazer, hitting Michael in the head twice, killing him instantly. He hit Carlos in his huge powdery white chest.

Tom sped immediately toward the park when he heard the shots. He was on the radio immediately when he saw what had happened. "Officer down! Shots fired! Code 9! Code 9!"

Tom arrived seconds later and found Joey holding his left shoulder, blood running down his arm. A puddle was already forming on the blacktop. Tom peered inside the Blazer and saw instantly that the driver was dead. The back of his head was splattered on the headrest. The passenger had blood oozing from his chest, and the big ugly guy was sitting perfectly still. Tom ran to his trunk and grabbed the first aid kit. After sprinting back to the Blazer, he started to apply direct pressure to the wound with a handful of bandages to stop the bleeding. Although Carlos looked to Tom as though he might be dead as well, he was still very much alive. While Tom's back was turned to the window, Carlos got off another very lucky shot that struck Tom just below the head. He was dead before he hit the ground. Joey swung around and emptied his weapon into the man's huge white chest. Joey dragged himself to his patrol car, repeated the Code 9 over the radio, and asked for medics and the first aid squad.

Within minutes, the area was crawling with police, emergency personnel, and the local media. Joey was ushered into the ambulance and taken to Monmouth Medical for treatment. Michael Power, Carlos Ferrer, and Officer Tom Brougham were pronounced dead at scene.

Chapter 13

THE 9 MM round had gone right through Joey's shoulder, causing a major muscle tear as well as a shattered rotator cuff. The physician told Joey that he would be out of work for at least seven months. However, Joey's worst pain was not physical; it was mental.

While Joey was in the hospital, a police officer guarded his door around the clock. The only people allowed in the room were family and other cops. Joey had no brothers or sisters, his father had died several years before, and his mother lived in Florida. Still, his mother called every night since the shooting. Noticeably, the only people who visited were police officers. Reinus the Anus came by to see him, along with the mayor. The chief brought his own photographer, who took a picture of him leaning over Officer Sabba, shaking his good hand while the mayor looked on. The whole incident made Joey feel sick, but at least the circus behavior took his mind off his throbbing shoulder. Joey knew the photo would eventually make it into the *Two River Times*, accompanied by an article about how the chief stood by his officers. The accompanying article would include a quote by Reinus the Anus on how he hoped Officer Sabba would have a quick and safe recovery and that the department would be anticipating his quick return.

Joey was released from the hospital three days later, just in time for Tom's funeral.

∧ ∧ ∧ ∧ ∧ ∧

Tom's body was being viewed at the Gibilisco & Lehrer funeral home located three blocks from Two River police headquarters. The huge old Victorian house was converted to a funeral home in the late sixties, and it still had all the original ornate characteristics that were included during its original construction in the late 1800s.

It was a Saturday morning, and Joey knew the funeral home would be jam-packed with people. Joey parked his car in the first available parking space, which was two blocks away, and even before he got out of the car, he felt the knot in his stomach start to tighten. As he walked toward the funeral home, he saw a long procession of Two River police cars stretched in front of the home, accompanied by other police cars from neighboring towns. Most of the vehicles were double-parked and blocked the westbound lane. Two young rookie cops in dress uniform with white gloves were standing in front of the driveway directing traffic and crossing the mourners. Joey gave them a wave and made his way to the front sidewalk. With his arm still in a sling, and wearing a black suit, he tried hard to prepare himself for the next couple of hours. Joey had no idea of what he was about to endure, and it was by far the worst day of his life. As he walked up the steps, he saw on the outside front porch a group of Tom's cousins and distant relatives, most of whom he'd met several times when Tom and Judy celebrated the birthday parties for Jason and Nicole. This time, however, there was no celebratory mood present. There was no storytelling, no jokes, and certainly no laughter. Instead, there were tears, tissues, and runny makeup. Joey attempted to walk around the group in an effort to remain unnoticed, but his good arm was suddenly seized by Melissa Fama. Melissa was Tom's close first cousin and godmother to his daughter, Nicole. Her eyes were bloodshot, and it looked as though she hadn't slept in days. Joey pulled her close and gave her a firm hug.

"I'm so sorry, Melissa. I know how close the two of you were."

Not wanting to disengage from their hug, Melissa said, "He was too young to die, Joey. He was a great father and husband. Why does God do such things to good people?" Her words were filled with despair, and she started to cry on his shoulder.

Joey held her until she settled down somewhat. Her words seemed to cut through his heart like a serrated knife, bringing back a flood of memories of Tom that he had tried desperately to keep buried since that night. The thought of the money slowly seeped into his conscience. It was like a hundred-pound weight that dangled around his neck; it was choking the life out of him by the second. Joey held back his own tears as Melissa's grip eased. She finally lifted her head and kissed him on the cheek.

"It will be all right," Joey said with as much conviction as he could muster. "If there is anything I can do, just ask."

"Thanks, Joey. I know the two of you were very close. Judy and the kids will sure be able to use a good friend like you," Melissa said with the saddest smile he had ever seen.

"Thanks, Melissa. I'll see you inside." He kissed her cheek and walked quickly through the front entrance.

Usually, the funeral house was partitioned; one huge room split into two smaller rooms that were used for separate funerals. But today, the funeral home was dedicated to just one service, and it was already packed. The overflow spilled out onto the front porch. There were beautiful flower arrangements on both sides of the casket, and they extended down both sides of the room. Joey made his way down the center hall, acknowledging people and shaking hands with fellow police officers as he walked toward the open casket. He felt a wave of nausea wash over him as he walked closer to Judy and her children, all dressed in black. Judy looked terrible but appeared under control. Nicole and Jason ran to Joey when they saw him.

"Uncle Joey," they shouted as they buried their teary little faces into his good shoulder.

Nicole looked up at Joey with her big brown eyes as if he might have an answer to her unasked question. She and her brother were just too young to lose a father, too young to understand what death was all about.

Joey knelt down in front of the casket, said a small prayer for Tom and a bigger prayer for himself, asking Tom to forgive him. He got up and gave Judy another hug and then got lost in the crowd. He left early and stopped at the first bar he found.

The next day at the cemetery, after the funeral service was over, Tom's wife walked up to Joey and thanked him for being such a good friend and partner. Joey walked away and vomited next to a tree. Captain Whitman walked up and put his hand on Joey's good shoulder.

"Sorry, Joe. I know you guys were close. C'mon, I'll get you out of here."

Chapter 14

JOEY WAS OUT of work, his arm in a sling, and the doctor had practically told him that he was not going to return to the department any time soon. "An indefinite period," he'd said. Because of that, it would be months before he returned, which would include light duty until he was completely healed.

Several days after Joey was released from the hospital, Captain Paul Whitman called Joey at home, asking how he was feeling. Captain Whitman was in charge of the detective bureau and the narc squad, and he was a good friend of Joey's. They had gone to the police academy together and had been on the force for the same amount of time. Paul was a big man, with a barrel chest with a crop of thick, bushy brown hair. He had earned the nickname Bear at the academy. As Paul moved through the ranks, the rookies knew not to call him by his nickname. They all addressed him as captain or just sir. Only Paul's good friends got away with calling him Bear, and Joey was one of them.

Joey and Paul got together about once a month and would usually go out to dinner or take a ride on his sailboat. Paul's wife, Donna, tried constantly to set Joey up with one of her divorced friends. Paul suggested they go to the Salt Creek Grille for dinner to discuss something important. Joey sensed urgency in Paul's voice and agreed to call him in the next couple of days.

Joey hung up the phone feeling like shit. He tried to cheat life and steal more than a million dollars that was not his. Since the accident just a week ago, his life was supposed to have changed for the better, but the money had done exactly the opposite. He no longer slept well at night since he could not forgive himself for his partner's death. He usually lay awake at night, haunted by the vision of Tom's wife, Judy, and the kids just as they were that day. They were huddled tightly together, their arms around each other crying, surrounded by family members, and all standing next to Tom's open casket.

His depression followed him constantly, and there was no cure any doctor could prescribe that would relieve his mental anguish. His temporary relief could be found in a bottle of vodka, and when he drank enough, it would numb his mind and let him forget. *If only I could go back in time. If only I had never taken the money. Money sucks. Sucks!* It was the last thing he thought as he swallowed the last sip from the bottle and passed out.

After three days of being drunk, alone, and withdrawn, Joey had to make a decision. *Do I become a self-pitying alcoholic and shoot myself, or do I do something about it?* His first thought, which would be the easiest, was to end it all. As they say in the business, he could eat his gun. It would be fast and would end the constant pain, the voices of guilt that played in his head like a broken record.

Chapter 15

IT WAS ELEVEN o'clock on a Tuesday morning, and Joey had straightened up his house, made the bed, cleaned the sink of dirty dishes, and threw away the empty bottles that had accumulated on every flat surface in the place. With a hangover and a wealth of mental anguish, Joey drove to the marina and set sail to the Sandy Hook Bay and toward the ocean, his forty-five Smith & Wesson strapped to his hip. There was some overcast, and as Joey looked up–as if nature was reading his mind, it appeared as though a black cloud was following him out to sea. *It won't be long now. Soon, I'll be at peace.* He motored slowly past the Sandy Hook Lighthouse, and ten minutes later, he was rounding Sandy Hook on his right, the Verrazano Bridge two miles to his left. Normally, Joey would stop and anchor to enjoy the view, but today's trip would be unlike any he had ever taken before. He sailed down the coast not looking at the view; his mind was focused on one thing.

Somewhere two miles off the coast between Monmouth Beach and Long Branch, Joey stopped the engine and went down into the cabin. His depression was being fueled by his guilt, which gave him the impetus to sit down and pull the pistol from its holster. Without thought or feeling, Joey raised the gun and turned the barrel so that it was facing him. He adjusted his hand so that his thumb was inside the trigger guard resting on the trigger. Joey opened his mouth and placed the cold steel barrel inside as his thumb started to pull back the trigger. Joey's mind flooded with memories of his childhood, old girlfriends, graduating the police academy, and his parents. His mother, who would never see him again, would never understand. His thumb pulled on the trigger in slow motion. He watched as the hammer moved back, almost to the point of release, where it would slam forward against the firing pin. Then there were more memories of his parents, back when he was a child, his first day of school, his first baseball game. He saw his mother kissing him on the cheek, telling him not to take things too seriously. She would always say that the two most important things in life were your health and family. Now the hammer had nowhere to go but forward. At the last possible second, Joey reached up with his left hand and managed to put his thumb between the hammer and the firing pin, stopping the gun from firing. He quickly pulled the weapon from his mouth, gently removed his thumb, and let the hammer down. He sat inside his cabin and cried.

After three days of sobriety, Joey was ready to confront his demons. Attempting suicide had opened his eyes. He knew he could be more useful to Tom's family and to himself if he helped the police department find the ones responsible for his partner's death.

Chapter 16

FIRST THING JOEY did was call Bear. Seeing Bear always cheered him up, and he could certainly use a little uplift. Bear eagerly accepted to meet Joey at the Salt Creek for dinner at eight o'clock.

Dinner at the Salt Creek was usually good, but anything Joey ate or thought about registered anything but good. Captain Whitman showed up a little after eight and saw Joey sitting at the bar with an empty martini glass in front of him. Paul ordered a scotch on the rocks and told the bartender to give Joey a refill. Joey had not been drinking these last couple of days and on an empty stomach, the martini went right to his head.

It was the only thing that calmed him down.

"I hope you're hungry," Paul said. "There's an hour wait, but I know the maitre d', and he'll sit us in a few minutes."

As the captain had forecast, the maitre d' collected the pair and escorted them to a window table overlooking the Navesink River and the Oceanic Bridge. Both men ordered a few minutes later and waited for their appetizers to arrive.

"Before I start with what I want to tell you, I want you to know that I personally investigated the shootings at Marine Park, as per the chief. Everything in your report reflected the chain of events that occurred." Bear stopped, cleared his throat, and took a sip of his drink before continuing, "However, your video camera and mic were off the entire time. The only audio and video I had were from Tom's camera, and it showed him arriving on the scene after most of the shots were fired. Unfortunately, the only video we have is Tom getting shot, and you unloading your gun inside the Blazer."

Joey cut in, "Everything happened so fast. The last thing on my mind was turning on the damn camera."

"C'mon, Joe, you know when you turn on your overheads for a vehicle stop, the camera automatically starts to record. Are you telling me that you pulled that car over without your lights on?"

"I didn't pull it over. It was parked in the lot after dusk. I pulled next to it just to advise them to move. I never thought–"

"Twenty years on the job. You should know better. Never take anything for granted," Bear said, finishing his drink.

"What now? Is the chief looking to suspend me again?" Joey asked.

"Relax, Joe. I took care of everything. The bad guys are dead. I closed the investigation. Case closed. That's all the chief needs to know."

Joey raised his martini glass. "Thanks, Bear. I owe you one."

"Forget it. You would have done the same for me," Bear said.

"You're right, but is that what you wanted to talk to me about?"

"No, there's something else," Bear said with a serious look on his face.

"Please no more bad news," Joey said, lifting his good arm as if surrendering.

For his part, Joey preferred, and tried hard, to forget about everything–his job, his partner, the money, and the Hilltop Corporation. He wished he could rewind his life to five minutes before the accident. He would never have taken the money.

"I had lunch with an old friend from the FBI yesterday," Paul said, "Agent Dave DeSordi."

Joey shrugged his shoulders, "And–So?"

Paul continued, "Dave told me that the feds have been investigating Dominick Zarza. They think he's involved in a multimillion-dollar drug trafficking ring."

"That's impossible," Joey said, completely surprised by the news. "Zarza's worth more than a billion dollars. Besides, he's politically connected with the mayor and governor. Why would he be involved in drugs?"

Paul had a hard time controlling himself. The chief didn't know about the information he had. "Dave says Zarza was involved in a big stock deal that went bad a couple of years ago. He lost most of his money–got swindled by some big-time stockbroker named Mark Keats. The FBI is trying to locate Keats as we speak because the SEC wants him for insider trading. Evidently, the guy violated all kinds of federal regulations. Right now, the FBI thinks he left the country with more than a hundred fifty million dollars. They're following the paper trail, which leads to Switzerland, but they think he's somewhere in Costa Rica."

Joey was taking in all of the information Paul was offering, not saying a word. He took a big gulp of his martini and sat up, finally interested in something other than his own guilt.

Paul continued, "The FBI and the DEA have been investigating Dominick Zarza for the last year and a half. Besides the loss he suffered at the hands of Keats, he has a cocaine dependency. In fact, Dave thinks he's dealing a lot of cocaine, possibly millions of dollars a month."

Paul stopped talking as the waiter served their appetizers, and Joey could not believe what he was hearing. With their food in front of them, it was clear to Joey that Paul was more in the mood to talk than eat.

"The FBI had set up a sting operation in Manhattan where some undercover Chinese agents made a buy from a couple of Zarza's dealers. Get this, the dealers' names were Tony Maisto and Vince Cimilucca, the very same knuckleheads who crashed on Route 88." Paul picked up a Buffalo chicken wing and sucked all the meat off in one swallow.

Joey played with his romaine salad, picking out an olive and throwing it into his mouth as if he had an appetite.

"You know how the FBI acts," Paul went on, "never wanting to share information with the local police. They wanted all the glory."

Joey nodded his head and said nothing.

"After the FBI made the deal with Maisto and Cimilucca, they put a tail on him. They wanted to follow the money. I think he said it was a million two for thirty-five kilos of coke. Well, the FBI screws up and loses the trail somewhere between Manhattan and Jersey. The dealers drive through Two River, and the FBI has no idea where they've been. They're not sure if they got rid of the money before the crash or if someone took the money after the crash." Paul hesitated for a moment, not wanting to say what was next. "The FBI thought your partner, Tom, might have taken the money, but they ruled him out after the shooting. They think the dirtbags you shot in Harbor Park had something to do with the money. The FBI lab confirmed that the cocaine that was found in their Blazer came from the same batch of cocaine found at the accident. After their screwup, the FBI is being cautious about who to blame."

Joey nodded in acknowledgement. "What about Zarza's political ties to the chief and mayor? Are they aware of his drug involvement?"

"I don't think so. Everything Dave told me is confidential. The chief knows nothing of my conversation with the FBI. As far as the chief and mayor are concerned, Zarza is still just a wealthy real estate developer." Paul shut up again as the waiter brought their entrées to the table.

Joey was beginning to feel a little better and ate a piece of his rare tuna steak.

"The FBI is fully aware of Zarza's political ties that go as far up as the governor," Paul said. "That's why they want to have all the evidence and a very strong case before they make any indictments. Losing the money trail was just a temporary setback."

Joey took a sip of his martini, looking a bit confused, and said, "Why are you telling me all this?"

"Because you're my friend and this asshole Zarza is responsible for shooting you in the shoulder and having your partner killed. You and I are the only ones in the department that have this information. I want you to be very careful in the future, Joe. This deal is far from over."

If he only knew the whole story, Joey thought. The conversation was bringing him down further than he could have ever imagined. "Thanks Paul, I appreciate you telling me and for your concern."

In reality, Joey wanted to sail his boat out to sea and never come back. The hole he was digging was getting deeper by the day, and there was no way out.

Paul noticed Joey's distraction. "Sorry, Joe, I keep forgetting how close the two of you were. I apologize for bringing up the subject again. I just thought you should know."

The waiter came with the check, and none too soon for Joey. He wanted to get out of there and run, hide, go someplace where no one knew him. He wished he could go back in time, before the police academy, when he was just a kid in school. He hated his job, his life, and most of all, the deceit that nowadays filled his being. He had become a traitor and a liar. He was worse than the criminals he put in jail. *How has my life gotten so bad so fast?* he thought.

As Paul was paying the bill, Joey wondered about something else that struck him oddly. It was something Paul had said about the money; the deal about it being just temporary setback. Joey wanted to ask the question when he heard it, but lost interest a second later. Now he remembered what he wanted to ask.

"Paul, one thing you said earlier," Joey said as they both started to stand. "You said that when the FBI lost the tail on the dealers and the money, that it was only a temporary setback."

"Yeah. That's what Dave told me," Paul said as he made his way back to the bar.

Joey chose his words carefully. "You said losing the money was a temporary setback. I would think that losing the money would be a very big setback in the FBI's investigation."

Paul sat at the bar and ordered them two more drinks. The vodka was starting to bring a little relief to Joey's guilt. Joey felt he could spend several more minutes inside the place before running out.

"Well, that's what you would think, but even though the FBI screwed up, those guys aren't stupid. Dave DeSordi told me the money they used in the sting was organized into hundred-dollar bundles of ten thousand dollars, all banded together using a unique money wrapper." Paul looked up to see if Joey was listening.

Joey was staring into his glass as if he wasn't concerned, but his mind hung on every syllable coming out of Paul's mouth.

"Do you follow me so far?" Paul asked.

Joey nodded his head, never looking up.

Paul continued, "They aren't ordinary money wrappers. All of them contain a long threadlike microchip that works as a GPS locator. So the FBI could locate the money any time."

Joey's heart almost stopped. *How much worse can this get? Maybe I should give up now. Tell Paul everything before the FBI tells him the money is on my boat.* Joey couldn't even look up. He was paralyzed, stunned at what he was hearing. Joey was losing it, paranoia closing in on him quickly; he figured it was only a matter of time before the FBI rushed in with handcuffs gleaming. *What if this whole meeting is a setup? Maybe Paul already knows I have the money and is working with the FBI. He's probably wired. This whole conversation is being taped by the FBI, and this guy Dave What's-his-name is waiting outside in a white van listening.* Joey jumped up from his stool, told Paul he had to take a piss, and ran to the bathroom. He went down a flight of stairs to the men's room and headed to the farthest compartment. Inside, he shut the metal door, locked it, and sat on the toilet seat. *I've got to calm down,* he said to himself. *If they knew I had the money, the FBI, along with Reinus the Anus, would have had me indicted and in jail by now. Get it together, the alcohol is making your mind crazy.* Joey took fifteen long minutes to compose himself before he went back to the bar. Before he did, he exited the restaurant from the bottom floor, checking the parking lot for a suspicious white van. When he didn't see one, he went back upstairs and sat next to Paul.

"You look like you saw a ghost!" Paul said, sipping his scotch and water. "Are you okay? We can leave now if you'd like. I'll drive you home, leave your car here."

Joey saw that Paul looked concerned.

"No, I'm okay," Joey said without conviction. He knew that he still had to ask the most important question of his life. He took a big swig of his martini and almost drained it. "If the FBI knows where the money is, why haven't they gone after the person who has it?"

"It's not that simple," Paul said, seeing the concentration on Joey's face. "The money wrappers will only set off a signal once they're ripped open. Once the wrapper is ripped and the filament is broken, it sets off a GPS signal, and the FBI can follow the money. It leaves them with plenty of options. Plus every bill is marked."

Joey felt a small moment of fleeting relief. He was thinking hard trying to remember how much he handled the money, confident that he hadn't damaged or removed any of the wrappers. The knot in his stomach began to loosen, and the loud voices in his head started to quiet down enough to allow him to absorb what Paul had just said. "Do you mean they don't know where the money is?" Joey asked as the color started to return to his face.

The bartender came by to ask if they needed a refill, and Paul held up two fingers. When the bartender left, Paul said, "I don't know. Agent DeSordi, even though he is a good friend, would only tell me so much. I've told you everything I know."

"Thanks, Paul, but I'm curious about why they didn't just put one of those microchips in the case the money was in? That must have been a lot of money, which needed to be carried in some type of case."

"I'm not really sure," Paul said, stirring the ice in his glass with his index finger. "The only reason I could think of is that Dave is a very controlling and analytical guy. I remember one case he told me about, which was similar to this one in terms of tracking drug money. They did a similar sting operation and only had the case that contained the money wired with a chip. After the dealers left, the agents gave them a couple of hours and followed the money to a deserted house on the outskirts of Newark. The agents went right inside, thinking the dealers would be there with the money, but the only thing they found was an empty case—no money, no dealers. It so happened that the dealers were watching the house as the FBI agents went inside. No arrests were made. The operation took two years of time and money."

"I guess DeSordi wants to make sure there is someone with the money when they locate it this time," Joey said.

"You bet your ass. He was almost demoted because of that case. Turns out it was two rookie agents who screwed it up for him, rushing into the house before any type of surveillance was conducted. They were trying to make names for themselves. They probably thought they'd go inside and find a group of drug dealers sitting around a table drinking beer and splitting up the money." Paul paused a second, taking a small sip of his drink, knowing he had Joey's full attention. "Drug dealers today are getting more sophisticated. You have to realize that these guys are making millions of dollars and can afford to buy the technology they need to detect any type of microchip that sets off a signal. DeSordi figured that that's exactly what happened in that sting operation. The dealers knew the bag was wired and left the FBI standing there with its thumb up its ass," Paul said, using a gesture. "You can bet Dave DeSordi will never let that happen again. He's out to get Zarza and anybody else who's involved."

Joey shook his head as the lightbulb went on and said, "So that explains the money wrappers. They don't set off any type of signal and can't be detected until they're ripped open."

"Exactly," Paul said as he finished his drink and started to get up from his bar stool. "Are you sure you don't need a ride home?"

"No thanks, I'm okay. And thanks again for dinner and the conversation."

"That's what friends are for," Paul said.

"Oh, one more thing," Joey added. "Does the FBI think anyone else is involved with Zarza?"

"I'm not sure. If there is, DeSordi was keeping it to himself."

"Thanks again, Paul."

"No problem, Joe. Go home and get some sleep. You look like shit. Oh, I almost forgot," Paul said.

What now? Joey thought.

"When you're up to it, I want to take you out on my new boat," Paul said, finishing the last of his drink.

"You finally splurged and bought your dream boat?" Joey asked, trying to share Paul's enthusiasm.

"It's a great boat. You're gonna be very surprised when you see it," Paul said, beaming.

"How big is it?"

"I'm not saying another word except that I named it the *Sea Bear*."

"I can't wait to see it. I'll call you soon."

They shook hands and left.

As Joey drove home, he thought that things were still all right considering what could have happened. The FBI did not know or suspect he had the money. The money was worthless, and he needed to get rid of it. He could fill the duffel bag with bricks and throw it overboard three miles off the coast. It would never be found, and eventually, everyone would forget *except Dominick, Judy, Nicole, Jason, and me.*

Joey drove over the Oceanic Bridge, looking at the huge mansions high on the Monmouth hills overlooking the Navesink River, and he immediately thought of Dominick Zarza. Joey knew he had to do something to get even; not for himself, but for his partner, Tom. He needed a plan.

Chapter 17

AT SEVEN O'CLOCK on Friday evening, Joey drove to the entrance of Dominick Zarza's mansion. The house, which was barely visible from the entrance, sat high on the hill. The west side sloped down in waves of green grass and huge oak trees were strategically placed to add to the already majestic appearance of the property. The entrance bordered a small dead-end street, which was only used by the residents of the mansion and the police that patrolled the area. About a hundred yards farther down was another entrance, which had a sign that read For Deliveries Only. The borders of the property were surrounded by a six-foot-high black fence, outside of which was a thick row of neatly sculptured hedges. The east side of the property jutted out three hundred feet and then stopped abruptly at a sizeable cliff that fell away a hundred fifty feet below. The house sat high in the Rumson hills overlooking the Shrewsbury River, the Atlantic Ocean, and Manhattan. Joey remembered a national home magazine that carried a huge article on the home, stating that it had the best view and location in Monmouth County if not the entire state of New Jersey. Joey sat inside his car at the front of the driveway, stopped by two large metal gates, each attached to its own massive stone pillar. The pillar to his left had an intercom system, and above, almost out of view, was a security camera. He glanced across and saw that one was attached to each pillar. Just as Joey reached out of his window to buzz the intercom, he heard a voice.

"Do you have an appointment with Mr. Zarza?"

Joey felt his adrenaline kicking in because of what he was about to do, and it prevented him from speaking for several seconds. He took a deep breath and finally said, "I don't have an appointment, but I'm sure Mr. Zarza would want to see me."

"Mr. Zarza is a very busy man. Leave your name, the nature of your business, or a business card in the metal box beneath the speaker, and if he's interested, someone will contact you." And the intercom went silent.

Joey pressed the intercom's button again, but it remained silent. He knew they were watching him, and he pressed and held the button until the voice came back.

"If you insist upon not leaving, we will have you removed."

Seconds later, Joey saw a black Blazer pulling up beside him that must have come from the delivery entrance. Soon enough, he was looking at two huge men staring back at him. Fortunately, he'd thought ahead and was wearing his bulletproof vest. His hand found the grip of his Smith & Wesson almost instinctively.

"Put your shit in the metal box and leave. You're trespassing on private property. This is your first and only warning!" The driver's tone was not as polite as the voice from the intercom.

Joey knew better than to argue with goons like these. He heard the crackling of a walkie-talkie from inside the goons' car and decided to forge ahead. "Listen, I don't want any trouble with you or anybody at this—"

"We know you don't so get lost before you have all the trouble you can handle," the driver said, not giving Joey time to finish speaking.

Joey had spent a career dealing with street thugs, and these guys were no different. They would follow anybody with some power and enough money to give them a paycheck. They were insignificant little soldiers, and obeying orders gave them a feeling of importance. Ignoring the driver, Joey said, "You have walkie-talkies in there so please contact the person inside and tell him that I need to talk to Mr. Zarza."

The driver finally lost his patience, and he started to get out of the vehicle. But the passenger, who had not yet spoken, reached across and kept him inside. The passenger, who had turned people away from the main entrance many times, had never experienced someone who clearly was not intimidated by two huge bodyguards. The passenger, Ziggy, leaned over toward the driver and said, "Maybe Mr. Zarza would want to see this guy?"

TJ, the driver, shrugged his shoulders. "Why would he want to see him? Mr. Zarza didn't recognize him from the security camera. Let's just get rid of him."

Ziggy turned toward the open window and said to Joey, "You know we can't just let you in. Give me your name, and I'll let them know inside. If Mr. Zarza does not want to see you, I'm going to let my friend TJ get out of the car and give you an education. You got that?"

Someone with half a brain, Joey thought. He knew he had only one chance to get inside, and time was running out. He looked straight into

Ziggy's eyes and said, "You tell Mr. Zarza that I'm the Two River cop who has his money." Joey paused, letting what he had just said hang in the air for a moment. Then added, "I don't think he is interested in my name."

Ziggy rubbed his chin with his right hand and said, "You have a lot of balls coming here all alone admitting you have the money. You must have a death wish?"

"Just give him the message," Joey instructed.

Ziggy whispered into the walkie-talkie, out of earshot of Joey, and twenty seconds later, the huge metal gates started to open.

Dominick watched both cars on his security camera as they made their way up the half-mile driveway. His concentration was focused on the driver of the first car, the dirty cop who stole his million dollars and killed two of his men.

Joey's hands were wet with sweat as he crested the hill and emptied into a huge circular driveway. From the entrance all the way to the top, the landscaping was impeccable. To his right side, down a smaller adjoining driveway, was a ten-car garage with arches supported by stone columns built in a semicircle. To Joey, it looked almost Romanesque, an imitation of the Roman Coliseum. To the left was a wide walkway that led toward two huge wooden doors that were probably fifteen feet high. Joey stopped the car and took a deep breath to calm himself before he actually–finally–started to do what he had planned. As he got out of his car, the two goons approached him and threw him on the hood of his car. Sharp pains ran through his shoulder and arm. They frisked his whole body head to toe, taking away his pistol.

"It's not every day we get a visitor who wears a bulletproof vest and carries a forty-five. You must have been looking forward to some excitement," Ziggy said sarcastically.

"Yeah, and when Mr. Zarza is through with him, I'll give him all the excitement he wants," TJ said eagerly to no one in particular.

Show me the rabbits, George, Joey thought when he heard the big goon speak again. *Dominick mustn't be too smart if he hires idiots like these. No wonder he lost all his money.*

They flanked Joey as they escorted him to the wooden doors, which opened as they approached. Joey knew someone was watching their every move. The man at the door was much older, a good deal smaller, and he looked much more cerebral than intimidating. Completely different from the two bookends glued to his sides. He was dressed casually and spoke softly.

"Come in, Mr. Sabba. Mr. Zarza is waiting for you in the study."

The entrance foyer was a massive semicircular room with four huge archways leading the way to four different directions. Joey figured the ceiling was at least forty feet high, and he noticed the colossal chandelier hanging from the center. The floor was black marble, probably imported from Italy. As the man turned, Joey sensed something very different inside. Even though the house was enormous and built with the most expensive materials, it was not as well kept as the façade of the house. Outside, every shrub and bush, every blade of grass was properly cut and manicured. But inside, the place looked dirty and disorganized. The chandelier looked like it hadn't been cleaned in years, and the marble floor hadn't been buffed clean in a long time. Joey thought of the conversation he had with Paul at the Salt Creek Grill. The FBI agent said that Zarza had lost most of his money in the stock market and was almost broke. You would never think it by the outside, but the interior told a different story.

Joey figured Dominick wanted to keep up his appearance as a wealthy entrepreneur, but doing so must have cost him greatly. *Dominick might need this money more than I figured,* Joey thought as he entered Dominick Zarza's study. *If Dominick was worth the billions he once had, I would have been dead by now.*

The room was massive and ornate like the foyer, and there was a strong smell of cigar smoke in the air. Worn leather furniture was scattered around the room, and to the right, sitting in a huge leather armchair behind a large oak desk, was Dominick Zarza. Hung on the wall to the side was a huge flat panel TV, and just below it was a small cabinet filled with a variety of electronics with rows of DVD movies piled randomly on top. In front of the TV sat a leather couch and a coffee table, the latter of which, Joey saw, was covered with empty pizza boxes and beer bottles. *I guess the maid and the chef are off today*, he thought as he was escorted to a seat in the front of Zarza's desk. Once there, he was shoved down; clearly, standing was not an option.

Dominick tilted his head toward the door, and the two goons started to leave the room.

"We'll be right outside the door if you need us, Mr. Zarza," TJ said as he turned to leave.

The doorman stayed and stood behind Dominick, his hands folded in front of him. Dominick did not look as he did in any of the pictures Joey had seen in the newspapers or those he'd seen on the wall in the chief's office. It looked like he'd lost weight, and his eyes were sunken deep into his head. His complexion was pale, as if he already had a foot in the grave. In the far corner of the desk sat a small grimy mirror with a rolled up bill beside it. *Someone with a bad cocaine habit,* Joey thought. On the other side of the desk sat a yellow file folder laid haphazardly, its papers looking outside at irregular angles. Joey strained to look closer and made out the black letters MPD stenciled on the cover. The pages sticking out looked incredibly like police report forms. It finally occurred to Joey that someone inside the department was giving Dominick all the information he needed.

Dominick picked up the cigar that was burning in the ashtray and stared at it for a long time. "First you steal my money, then you kill two of my men, and then you come to my house to tell me you stole a million dollars of mine. Give me one good reason why I shouldn't kill you right now and dump your body twenty miles offshore."

Joey was ready for what was happening; he'd rehearsed every word–every move–in his mind many times. He even managed to work up a thin smile. "Because if you kill me, you'll never get the money, which I am prepared to return, by the way."

"It costs me a million just to open my eyes in the morning! Do you think I would keep you alive for a lousy million dollars? If so, you're mistaken," Dominick bellowed as he puffed his cigar.

Joey's gut feeling was that Dominick was bluffing. He was obviously broke and needed the money badly. At the same time, he was a loose cannon, and there was no telling what he was capable of doing. Joey had to navigate the water cautiously and choose his words carefully. *Let him think he is in control. Give him all the power and get him to take the money.* Joey looked Dominick straight in the eyes and said, "Mr. Zarza, I have come here with the best intentions–to give back what I took. If I had any idea the million dollars was yours," Joey paused a moment, took a breath, and then continued, "I would never have taken it." *I would have come here and locked up your fat ass.* "Your family goes way back in this community and has helped a lot of people with charitable contributions. I know you are good friends with my chief, and I wouldn't want to do anything to interfere with that." Joey stopped before he made himself sick. He couldn't believe the bullshit he was saying.

Dominick sat up a little straighter in his chair. Obviously, he was enjoying what he was hearing. He leaned forward and said, "You'll have to pay for killing Michael and Carlos, the two guys you and your partner gunned down in the park."

Joey thought he had been making progress, but it appeared Dominick already had his mind made up. He realized he was being played with like a cat plays with a mouse. Joey knew he couldn't argue with him; it would do more harm than good. In addition, it was obvious Dominick didn't give a shit about those two thugs.

"Well, I'm sorry about your two associates. It was unfortunate that they were killed, and unfortunate that my partner was killed. I am here because I want to put an end to everything. I want my partner's wife and children safe, and I promise you that after you get your money, I'm going to retire from the police force," Joey said as he grew deadly tired of kissing the guy's ass.

Dominick put his cigar back in the ashtray and looked at Joey. "How would it look if I just let you walk out of here? I would lose respect from my family." It was Dominick's best imitation of the Godfather.

Respect, family, where the hell was that coming from? Joey thought, his temper building and his voice sharpening. "Listen, Dominick. I tried to do the right thing. If you want to kill me, go ahead, I really don't give a shit. Two days ago, I sat with my gun in my mouth ready to pull the trigger. I came a split second away from blowing the back of my head apart. Call in your two goons and take me away. You'll be doing me a big favor."

Dominick's mouth fell open slightly at the tirade, and Joey stood up, his voice booming. "Here's the deal. You meet me at Pirate's Cove tomorrow afternoon at two-sharp-tomorrow. Bring a wireless laptop and someone who knows how to use it, and you'll get your money. Oh, and be prepared to wire a hundred fifty thousand to an offshore account of my choice."

"What? Are you fucking crazy?" Dominick exploded, slamming his fist on the desk. "Why in the world would I wire you a hundred and fifty thousand dollars?"

Ziggy opened the office door, looked in for several moments, and saw that everything was under control, then closed it again.

"Just hear me out," Joey said insistently. "If you don't like what I have to say, have your goons haul me away."

Dominick looked up and took the cigar from his mouth, his breathing too labored to puff on it. He turned to the elderly man standing behind him, as if he was looking for guidance. The elderly man nodded his head slowly, approvingly, and Joey took it as a sign to continue.

"When I arrived at the accident, there was more than a million dollars in the duffel bag." Joey paused and stared into Dominick's eyes. "There was a hundred fifty thousand dollars more in the bag, which I believe your trusted associates were taking for themselves. I'm sure you would have found out eventually, and their fates would have been the same. I intend to give you all your money."

"But you want me to wire a hundred and a half large to your overseas account. Why didn't you just keep the 150K for yourself?" Dominick asked.

"Two reasons. First, you probably would have found out, and then my life would be threatened again. I don't want to have to look over my shoulder for the rest of my life. Plus, I doubt you would give me a second chance—"

Dominick interrupted, "I haven't given you a first chance yet, Sabba."

"May I continue?" Joey asked.

Dominick nodded slightly.

"And secondly, I am retiring and leaving the country. I do not want to risk traveling with the money and getting caught by customs or the IRS."

"If you leave, where do you plan to go?"

"Someplace where it's warm and cheap. I really haven't decided yet."

Dominick looked at Joey for a very long time and asked, "Why didn't you go through with it?"

"What do you mean?" Joey asked confused.

"Suicide. What stopped you?"

For the first time, Joey spoke from his heart, "Because I thought of my mother. She saved my life."

Deep down, Dominick felt his own pain again. He'd been lost since his mother died. Dominick could not go there. The need for cocaine immediately surfaced–a habit he had acquired to keep his insecurities hidden, a mechanism that kept his childhood in the dark. Dominick had frequent mood shifts, and this was one of them. He needed to be alone.

Joey saw the dramatic and immediate change in Dominick's demeanor.

Dominick called his two goons into the room. "Take him to his car and make arrangements to get the money. I want to be left alone."

Joey knew he was pushing the envelope but had to ask, "Who is the man behind you?"

Dominick looked up and answered without hesitating, "This is Sergio. He's been with my family since I was a small child. He is my closest and trusted friend."

Joey walked to the door with TJ and Ziggy following behind. As they exited the huge doors onto the walkway, Joey was relieved to see his car parked where he had left it. He turned to TJ, who appeared angry and frustrated, and said, "Can I have my gun back?"

TJ shot back instantly, "You're lucky you walked out alive and we–"

But Ziggy interrupted and told TJ to give him the gun. Reluctantly, TJ pulled the pistol from his waistband and gave Joey the gun.

"Does Mr. Zarza own a boat?" Joey asked Ziggy.

Ziggy seemed puzzled by the question, but that didn't prevent him from answering, "Yeah, he's got two of 'em."

"Is one equipped with a wireless computer with access to the Internet?"

Ziggy was close to putting an end to the stupid questions, but his curiosity overpowered him. "Sure. Mr. Zarza has a forty-two-foot Silverton with all the latest gadgets. There's a computer system on board that has a wireless modem."

Joey was pleased that Ziggy had some knowledge of computers since it would be an asset when they met tomorrow. "Good," Joey said, "I think it would be a good idea"–he paused a moment and thought, *Slow down, Joey, you're doing good right now*– "if it's okay with Mr. Zarza, we'll meet tomorrow at Pirate's Cove on the Navesink River tomorrow to exchange the money by boat. Also, could you give me a cell number? I'll give you a call to set up a time."

"Why by boat?" Ziggy asked.

"Because it would be a lot safer for me. Oh, and make sure he brings a dinghy, the river can get pretty shallow in certain areas."

Ziggy gave him a confused stare, but he also gave him a cell number, which Joey burned into his memory. After he left, Joey realized that Dominick was not a hard-core criminal or a bloodthirsty killer. Instead, he was a lonely, frightened billionaire whose life went totally astray because of bad business decisions and untrustworthy relationships.

Chapter 18

IT WAS EARLY, but the sun was already starting to burn through the morning clouds. Joey awoke, his eyes opening instantly, and he feels the anxious energy that instantly began to flow through his body. *Today should put an end to at least part of my problem,* he thought. Give the money back to Dominick and let the FBI take over. Let them make the big bust. They'll knock down his front door with a no knock warrant and drag him out with cuffs and leg shackles. After the arrest, the news will be leaked to the press, and it will be viewed on all the national and cable television networks. Too bad the chief can't take the credit. *But I'll make sure he has something else to worry about.* Joey was set on giving the money back, and afterward, he would try and get his life back into some semblance of order. He knew it would never be the same as before that wreck, but he would do everything possible to right the wrong he had committed. He knew he would never forgive himself for his partner's death due to his greed for money or for losing sight of what his job was all about. To protect and serve was the job description, and he had disgraced himself and the profession. He was a dirty cop, and his close friend had paid the ultimate price. His children were left without a father, his wife without a husband. Joey was trying to stay focused but was having a difficult time of it. In a split second, he made a very wrong decision, but Joey knew he could not change the past. It was the future that counted, and after today, hopefully, he would feel a little better. He wanted to get to the marina early before it got crowded.

As he pulled into the parking lot, he could tell by the number of cars that the weekend bennys were already packing up their boats with food, drinks, and fishing equipment, getting ready to cause havoc on the waterways. They never observed the no-wake zones, causing the boats in the marina to spring back and forth while tied to the boat lines. *Where are the marine police when you need them?* Joey thought. He walked through the lot toward the marina, carrying his Smith & Wesson and a wireless laptop computer. He had set up an offshore account earlier in the week, and the account number and password were embedded in his memory. In a few hours, Dominick would have all the FBI's marked and traceable money except for the 50K that he would mail to the chief, from Dominick, as a charitable donation. Joey intended to mail it after he finished the transaction at Pirate's Cove. *Let the chief talk his way out of this one.* When the dust had settled, Joey would have a hundred fifty thousand dollars in untraceable money resting quietly in an offshore account through which he could set up a trust fund for Nicole and Jason. So far, everything was going as planned.

Joey approached the sailboat and noticed a small group of guys and girls hanging out behind his neighbor's boat, obviously getting ready to party. Three of the guys had beer bottles in their hands, and four of the women were holding martini glasses with something red in them. Joey tried to sneak inside his cabin without being noticed, but it didn't work.

"Kind of early for you to be out, isn't it, Joe?" John, the boat's captain, yelled out. He stepped across and shook Joey's hand. "I've been following the newspapers and heard about your partner. We're all real sorry. If there's anything I can do, just ask."

"Thanks, John, I appreciate it. Tom was a good man." The wave of sadness passed over Joey like a wet blanket.

"Listen, Joe, if you'd like, if you feel like it, why don't you join us? We're waiting for one more—one you might be interested in, very cute and single." John lowered his voice so the others couldn't hear.

"I appreciate it, John, but no thanks. Another time. I have a lot of shit to do today."

Joey walked down the steps to the galley, but he had a feeling that John might try to persuade him one more time. He needed to get the boat moving as quickly as possible. The gas gauge read full, his sails were rolled in, and the motor started without hesitation. Joey united the lines and slowly motored out of the slip toward the Shrewsbury River.

Even though it was early, there was already a small flotilla of boats bobbing their way out toward Sandy Hook and then on to the open water. Inside the bay, the windsurfers and jet skiers tried to stay out of the way—and all too often dodge—the powerboats speeding past. Joey took his time and motored east, hugging the south side of the Navesink River and passing the turn for Pirate's Cove. Joey wanted to cruise past Dominick's mansion. It was close by, and with all the boats on the water, he would go unnoticed.

The farther he went, the higher the hills grew along the riverbank. Up high, in the Monmouth Hills, were some of the most expensive homes in New Jersey. Jon Bon Jovi lives in one of those mansions, and so did Geraldo Rivera. However, it was rumored that Geraldo sold his house a few years ago for nine million dollars due to a divorce. The person who bought it knocked it down and built a twenty thousand-square-foot castle. No one really knew if the money part was accurate, but the new house where Geraldo once lived was an obvious landmark to anyone on the river. It was also said that when Geraldo lived there, the bennys would anchor and look at his house through binoculars. One day, Geraldo became annoyed enough at the bennys that he walked to his dock overlooking the river, turned his back, pulled down his pants, and bent over.

Joey cruised past where Geraldo used to live and veered his boat around a bend. The hills on land had become steadily steeper, and the highest point of the cliff was where Dominick lived. The fortress sat high up and was set back far enough so that it was not visible from the river. The only part of the house that could be seen was the spire on one of the turrets, which rose seventy-five feet into the sky. The rest of the house was left to the imagination. Joey positioned the sailboat on the far side of the river. If there was anyone watching from on top of the cliff, he would go unnoticed due to the parade of boats, mostly heading east. A set of wooden steps was built from the top of the cliff to the bottom and halfway down, they emptied onto a small platform. Beyond that, they continued to the bottom, where they led to a huge deck and boathouse. Alongside the long staircase were two metal tracks with side rails that looked amazing like a set of railroad tracks. On the top of the tracks sat a railcar that was positioned on top of the cliff. Joey figured it as an electric car that would transport Dominick to and from his boat. Perpendicular to the deck was a fifty-foot pier that jutted out, which had a floating dock and six boat slips.

From across the river, Joey could see Dominick's Silverton tied to the end of the dock, the name CARMELA in big letters across the transom. On the other side of the dock, inside one of the other slips, was another boat. Joey knew Dominick had two boats, but Ziggy had told him that the smaller boat was a twenty-five-foot Sea Ray. Joey grabbed his binoculars and focused in on the other boat. It was smaller, but not by much, maybe a couple of feet. Joey zoomed in closer and saw 402 Luhrs printed on the side. Joey had a feeling he'd seen the boat before, but then many of the newer boats had the same design. But the feature that caught his eye was the wide blue metallic racing stripe that ran the length of the hull. It too reminded him of something, but he couldn't place it. Joey wanted to get a better look to be able to see the name. He moved farther down the river, and though he had increased his distance from the boat, he was able to come about and face the aft end of the Luhrs. He looked through his binoculars and moved them slowly to the stern and beneath the cabin. Then he focused in on the black letters across the transom. He couldn't believe what he saw. The words *Sea Bear* practically shouted at him. What was Paul doing at Dominick's place? And why was he there today?

Joey's mind was racing. That night at the park, Dominick's goons had all the information they needed about him and Tom's: home phone numbers, cell numbers, addresses, their cars–probably their shoe sizes too. Then Joey recalled seeing the official police reports on Dominick's desk the night before. No, he argued with himself. It couldn't be Paul! He'd been good friends with Paul for twenty years. Was he working with Agent DeSordi and the FBI? The situation made no sense at all. If Paul was in with Dominick, Joey thought, then he knew who had the money. But the money was worthless. Or was it? Joey needed more time. There were too many unanswered questions. He turned, came about again, and headed out toward the Navesink River. Fortunately, he still had a few more hours before the meeting.

He needed to figure out if the Bear was involved. He knew Paul's schedule by heart. He worked Monday through Friday and never on weekends unless there was a homicide or a hostage situation for which he could be called in by the chief. But those were rare occasions. Joey was near Barnacle Bill's, a local bar on the Rumson side of the river, which was very popular with the locals. He found a vacant slip that was used for dock-and-dine customers and tied up. Time was critical, and he didn't have much. He went down the steps to the cabin and unlatched the windows. The sun was rising along with the heat and humidity, and it was already near stifling below. Joey pulled his laptop from its case, turned it on, and placed the phone card into the proper slot. Within minutes, he was logged on to the Internet. A few clicks later, the FBI's home page filled his screen. From there, he located the New Jersey branch office in Newark along with its address and phone number. Joey could have called headquarters for a more direct number, but he didn't want his phone conversation taped. He wrote down the number, grabbed a handful of quarters from a jar on the counter, and walked to the pay phone in Barnacle Bill's parking lot.

The parking lot was half-full, but in another hour, every single space would be taken, and there would be a waiting line stretching outside the front door. Joey dropped a quarter into the coin slot and dialed the number, hoping a live person would answer the phone; he was in no mood to listen to a machine rattling off a long menu of options. After a few rings, an operator came on the line and told him to deposit another dollar and a quarter for five minutes. Joey dropped the money into the slot, and the phone rang three more times.

"Hello, this is the FBI office, Newark branch. My name is Suzanne. How can I help you?"

A real person! "Hi, Suzanne. My name is Peter, and I need to get in touch with one of your agents. Can you can connect me to his voice mail so I can leave him a message?"

"We have about two hundred fifty agents assigned to this office, Mr . . . . um . . ."

"Call me Peter."

"Okay, Peter. Well, like I said, we have quite a few agents here. What is this in reference to?"

"I'm sorry, but it's confidential. I was advised not to speak to anyone other than him."

"What's the agent's name?"

"Agent Dave DeSordi."

"Didn't the agent give you a contact number?"

"Yes, he did, but I can't locate it. Trust me, I wouldn't be bothering you if it wasn't important. And I believe Agent DeSordi would be very grateful if he received my message."

"How do you spell the name?"

"D-e-s-o-r-d-i," Joey said, breathing a sigh of relief.

"Hold on, please," Suzanne said, before the phone went silent.

Joey knew his five minutes were almost up, so he added five quarters. After several long minutes, the phone clicked on, and Suzanne's voice was back.

"I checked our listing for DeSordi, and we have no agent by that name."

It was exactly what Joey did not want to hear. "Are you sure? It's very important."

"I checked our entire database. I'm positive there isn't an agent here by that name. Can I help you with anything else?"

"Yeah, maybe. Could you give me the number to the New York City FBI branch?" Joey thought DeSordi must be from New York.

After Joey got the number, he hung up and dialed. Just like at the New Jersey office, he was informed that no agent by that name existed. Confused, Joey headed back to the boat, trying to piece the puzzle together.

If there's no Agent DeSordi, then there's no FBI investigation. All that bullshit Bear was passing about the money wrappers was a bunch of shit. The money isn't marked either. Slowly, things were starting to make sense for Joey. Bear wanted him to believe the money was worthless and that the FBI was closing in fast so he wouldn't have any reason not to return it to Dominick immediately. In fact, it gave Joey all the reasons why he should get rid of it as soon as possible. *How much was the Bear in for?* he wondered. How much control did he have over Dominick? Bear liked to be in control. He micromanaged his detective bureau, and nothing got by his desk without his approval. He personally checked and read every police report generated by the police desk. The rookies nicknamed him Mr. Mom behind his back. Joey had no choice but to figure that the Bear was in on it and that Dominick had told him about their meeting today.

Chapter 19

Joey CALLED PAUL'S cell phone; he needed to talk with him face-to-face. Luckily, Paul picked up on the first ring.

"Hello."

"Paul, this is Joe. We need to talk."

"You okay?"

"I'm fine," Joey said, immediately thinking about Sergeant Sherman's definition of FINE, *Fucked-up, Insecure, Neurotic, and Evasive.* "I need to talk to you about our conversation the other day. But I'd prefer to discuss this in person. Can we meet somewhere?"

"Sure. No problem, Joe. I'm out in my new boat. Why don't we go for that ride I promised you?"

"Okay. I'm docked behind Barnacle's. If you're not too far off, come and pick me up," Joey said, trying to add some excitement to his voice.

"That works for me," Paul answered. "I'm just ten minutes away."

Yeah, coming from Dominick's house. "I'll be here," Joey said as he closed his cell phone.

Joey went back aboard and climbed down into the cabin. He rummaged through several drawers and finally found what he was looking for. He placed it in his right pocket, finally happy that his oversized cargo shorts had several useful pockets. Then he secured the Velcro flap over the pocket. He looked down and checked the outside of the pocket, satisfied that the outline was unnoticeable.

Joey waited anxiously, not knowing how this next turn of events would turn out. The one thing he did know was that after his boat ride with Bear, he would have all of the pieces to the puzzle. Hopefully, Bear would have a good explanation for being at Dominick's, and everything would make sense. That way, the meeting he'd set up with Dominick would go as planned.

The more he thought about it, the more he couldn't believe Bear was involved. A captain in the Two River PD involved in one of the biggest drug operations in the country? How could he do it? Why would he do it? *How could I have done what I did?* They had been friends for years, and Joey never picked up an indication about Bear's involvement. He made more than a hundred thousand dollars a year, and his only son was almost finished with college. The boat must have cost at least three hundred thousand, which was within his means. He'd purchased his house twenty-five years ago and probably had no mortgage remaining. In fact, Bear never complained about money problems. Joey removed his gun and placed it inside the well-hidden compartment, locked the cabin, and stood on the dock. Ten minutes later, the sound of alarms and red flashing lights could be heard and seen from the Oceanic Bridge. Just like a train crossing an intersection, two arms decorated with flashing lights rotated around and blocked traffic in both directions. In the middle of the bridge just below the channel, two large steel gates seemed to split in half, each side rising slowly. The drivers of the cars parked on the bridge had exited their vehicles to watch the boats sail underneath. In the distance beyond the opened bridge, Joey could see the forty-foot Luhrs, its large white frame slicing gracefully through the water and glistening in the summer sun. The Luhrs's soaring outriggers were pointing upward, forcing the bridge to open so that it could pass underneath. Joey felt the outside of his pocket, making sure the small rectangle outline was not noticeable. To make sure, he crumpled a couple of napkins and placed them in the same pocket.

The *Sea Bear* was passing under the bridge and would be there in minutes, and Joey hoped Bear would arrive alone. It would be hard to imagine that anyone else from the department was involved. Even though Bear was an experienced captain, a forty-foot boat was difficult for one person to handle. As the *Sea Bear* came closer, Joey saw only one big bushy head atop the bridge.

Chapter 20

BEAR HANDLED THE forty-foot Luhrs like a pro, navigating through the tiny channel markings toward Barnacle Bill's marina. There was still an open spot in front of his sailboat, and Joey lifted his left hand over his eyes to block the sun. As he did, he felt the lingering soreness of the gunshot wound, aggravated the night before when Dominick's thugs frisked him. Still, he reached even higher and motioned toward Bear to pull in front. As the *Sea Bear* pulled in, Bear climbed down from the flybridge and threw Joey a line. Joey grabbed it and secured the heavy nylon rope immediately to the large, big metal cleat on the floating dock. He then headed toward the bow. Bear was already standing there with the next line, and he pitched that one to Joey as well. Standing in a slight crouch, Joey pulled the boat closer to the dock and tied the rope tightly to the cleat. He glanced aboard as he finished, and he was pleased when it appeared that Bear was the only one aboard. Joey spun back toward the stern and pulled himself on deck. Bear met him with a big smile and a strong hug.

"Good to see you, Joe. I hope everything is okay," Bear said, looking straight into his eyes.

Joey peered back into Bear's eyes, trying to read something—anything—but Bear's contagious smile was sincere, and Joey could do nothing other than smile back. He thought briefly again about how long they had been good friends, feeling guilty for even thinking Bear was involved in some major drug deal. "I'm fine, don't worry. I just wanted to ask you a few questions about the information you gave me the other night at the Salt Creek. But first, why don't you give me the guided tour of your new toy, it looks great."

Bear took a step back, but kept both hands on Joey's shoulders. "You're going to love it. This is my dream come true," Bear said, beaming.

"Well, let's get started. I want to see how the rich live," Joey said as he stepped back and freed himself from Bear's grip on his left shoulder.

"Sorry, Joe. I forgot about the shoulder," Bear said, his smile replaced by a look of concern.

"No big deal, it's feeling better every day. I go for rehab three times a week, you know. Doctor says I have a good chance of getting 70 percent mobility back in half a year or so, and then maybe I can get back to work on full duty."

"Well, enjoy the time off. I think it's best that you treat the whole thing as a vacation rather than an injury leave," Bear replied, trying to sound convincing.

"Easy for you to say. I don't mind the time off or the sore shoulder." Joey paused and looked into Bear's eyes and chided himself to choose his words carefully. "It's just that Tommy still consumes every thought. I could have saved his life if things were done differently."

"The worst thing that you can do is blame yourself. It wasn't your fault. My best advice to you is to grieve his loss: accept it, embrace it, and digest it. Then and only then will you be able to let it go," Bear said as he motioned Joey to sit on the white cushioned seat that stretched across the aft end of the boat. As Joey sank into the soft cushion, Bear disappeared into the cabin and came out holding two bottles of beer. He handed one to Joey and said, "To us and your partner, Tommy."

"To us," Joey repeated. They tapped their bottles together and sipped their beers as they had done many times before.

Bear gulped his beer down before Joey had time to take another sip. "C'mon, Joe, let me give you the tour. We'll start from the top of the flybridge and work our way down."

"You're the captain, Captain," Joey said, smiling. He was desperately trying to convince himself that Bear couldn't be involved. But then he thought, *Bear probably thinks it would be impossible for me to have taken the money in the first place.*

Bear headed back into the cabin and came out moments later holding a rocks glass filled with ice and a golden liquid. "Follow me, lad, you are about to see one hell of a boat."

Joey followed behind, thinking that the boat must have cost a small fortune, especially as they climbed the steps to the top of the flybridge twenty feet above the cabin. The bridge was a small command center that contained all the controls to drive the boat. It stood high above the cabin and gave Joey the feeling of being outside on a small balcony of an oceanfront condo overlooking the water.

Bear continued to narrate the tour as he sipped his scotch, never skipping a beat. He described how the boat had all the latest technology and how he could drive and dock the boat while perched high up in what he called the Seagull's Nest. It was hard for Joey to believe that such a small steering wheel and two small levers were capable of maneuvering the mass beneath them. As Bear finished talking, he noticed his glass was empty, except for the ice cubes that never had time to melt. It was time for another refill. They climbed back down the steep steps and into the cabin, which was equipped with a full kitchen and a medium refrigerator. Bear walked straight to the counter and poured himself another Johnny Walker Black on the rocks.

"The nectar of the gods," Bear said, holding his drink high as if toasting his boat.

"This is definitely living in style," Joey said, hoisting his half-full bottle of beer.

"Let's go. There's much more to see," Bear said as he walked down a small passageway, pointing out a full bathroom to the right and a large bedroom that was straight ahead. From the open door, Joey could see a queen-sized bed with a dresser, a full mirror, and a forty-two-inch plasma TV, complete with a Bose stereo system. Bear walked into the bedroom and motioned for Joey to come in, but he declined.

"Bear, if you want to get me into bed, you're going to have to try a lot harder than that," Joey said with a grin.

"I thought the boat would have been enough, but you always play hard to get. A few more drinks might do it," Bear said, laughing at his own reply.

"I think you're in desperate need of a wild woman," Joey said, sipping his beer.

"If you only knew the half of it," Bear said with a blank stare. It was an expression Joey had never seen before.

As they walked back toward the cabin, Joey noticed a closed door across from the bathroom. "What's this room?" Joey asked as he went for the doorknob.

Bear quickly grabbed his wrist and prevented him from opening the door. "Nothing in there worth seeing, really. Just a big storage room filled with life preservers, Jet Skis, and diving equipment. It's all piled up in one big mess."

Bear kept a firm grip on Joey's wrist until he let go of the knob.

"Let's go, I need another drink. Then I'll show you the ultimate command center," Bear said, waiting for Joey to take the lead into the cabin.

Joey knew Bear could drink, probably more than anyone he knew, but today, Bear was holding a pace he'd never seen before. He mixed another drink while Joey continued to nurse his first beer. Bear led Joey out of the cabin and turned right toward a small set of steps that curved left to another door. Bear walked inside to another console that looked similar to the one on the flybridge, except it was bigger, had more gadgets, and came complete with three big monitors.

Bear's eyes beamed. "This is where you want to be if the weather gets shitty or the seas get rough."

"What are these monitors for?" Joey asked, knowing Bear was having a great time showing off his boat.

"This one here," Bear said, pointing to the first monitor, "is the latest GPS system. It will tell you where you want to go, where you've been, where to eat, and even where to get laid. All you have to do is plug in the coordinates, and the autopilot will take you there. The only thing this can't do is give you head."

"Give it time," Joey said, realizing that the booze was putting Bear at ease. "With this toy of yours, you'll always be able to find a willing pair of lips. How about this one?"

"Ahh, my favorite. This middle monitor actually does four different things. It works as a radar unit, a depth finder, a fish locator, and a system that monitors all aspects of the boat, from the performance of the twin diesel engines to the temperature in the refrigerator."

"Wow, technology has come a long way."

"As you know, it all comes with a price, Joey," Bear said in a condescending tone.

Joey let it go, figuring the Johnny Walker was taking effect. He pointed to the last monitor in the trio, which was turned off.

"That's just a television hooked up to a satellite dish. It has no special function," Bear said as he headed for the cabin door, holding the glass he'd just drained.

"Can you grab me another beer?"

"You coming?" Bear asked.

"Nah, I'll be down in a second. I just like the feel of sitting in the captain's chair."

Bear let out a small laugh. "I'll be right up with your beer, sir."

This boat must have cost a fortune, Joey thought as he began to wonder about his meeting with Dominick. If Bear was involved and knew about it, he sure didn't seem to be in much of a hurry. Joey gazed at all the equipment and turned on the third monitor to catch the news. As the monitor came alive, the screen was divided into six separate smaller screens. Joey looked closer at the six different squares and couldn't believe what he saw. In the top left screen, he saw Bear in the kitchen pouring another scotch. The top middle was the rear cabin, and the top right was Bear's bedroom. The next screen, which didn't look familiar, was the room Joey hadn't seen–the one Bear obviously didn't want him to see. In reality, it was another bedroom. It was dark inside, but light enough that Joey could just make out the shape of a person lying on the bed. The other two screens showed views of the water from the forward and aft ends of the boat. Joey's eyes darted back and forth from the dark figure to Bear, who was still in the kitchen. He tried his best to make sense of the last twenty minutes. He knew there had to be an explanation. What was Bear hiding? Who was in the room? Joey watched Bear grab a beer out of the refrigerator before he headed for the steps. Joey quickly turned off the monitor, and Bear came in just a few seconds later. He was smiling and handed Joey his beer.

"Now that you've had the tour, let's take it for a little ride. It's amazing how smooth this baby is on the water. Why don't you go down and untie the lines, and I'll start the engines."

The sun was climbing higher, and there wasn't a cloud in the sky. Normally, this would be a perfect August day being out on the water, taking a ride on his good friend's new boat. But today wasn't that perfect day. Everything in Joey's life had turned upside down, and things seemed to be getting worse by the minute. Joey knew he had to learn the truth, so he untied the lines from the dock, hopped aboard, and signaled to Bear that they were clear. Bear notified the Oceanic Bridge to open as they left Barnacle Bill's and cruised toward the Sandy Hook inlet. The Luhrs cut through the water like butter. Joey sat in the rear of the open cabin on one of the cushioned seats and gazed out over the stern as the two powerful diesels churned through the water, forming a huge rooster tail in their wake.

After a twenty-five-minute ride past Sandy Hook and to the east of the Leonardo Pier, Bear continued southeast, farther down the coast and farther away from land. They passed two huge oil tankers that were headed for the New York harbor. They appeared to be standing still as the *Sea Bear* sped past doing about thirty knots. The *Sea Bear* cut through the water effortlessly, and the coastline was becoming visibly smaller by the minute. Joey realized that if Bear continued this course, they would lose sight of land entirely in a few more miles and be surrounded only by the vastness of the ocean and the infinite horizon beyond. The longer the trip lasted, the worse Joey felt in his gut. He had a sixth sense that would always raise his internal antenna if things were about to go bad. He couldn't count the number of times on the job when his gut feeling had saved him or his partner from a dangerous situation. It always told him either to be patient and wait, or to charge full steam ahead and not look back. The difference between his gut feeling now and the other times was that he was dealing with a good friend, someone he'd known for years. He was not dealing with a dangerous criminal on the street or with the unknowns associated with a routine traffic stop in which the driver could be a cold-blooded killer who was ready and happy to shoot him. Somehow, his sixth sense was telling him something different from what his emotions were feeling.

The events of the last few weeks flashed through his mind. How could he have taken the money? Why did his partner have to get shot, leaving two beautiful children and a devastated wife behind, all because of his greed? He'd dealt with street hoodlums, negotiated with criminals, and almost committed suicide. In a split second, his life had changed forever. He had always been reasonably happy with his life, never so depressed that suicide had ever entered his mind. Now he sat in his good friend's boat, not at all sure that his life would be spared. One thing he did know was that he needed to find out where Bear stood. He had to find out if he was in with Dominick and had made up the story about Agent DeSordi so that he would give the money back to Dominick in fear of ultimately getting busted. Was that Bear's plan? Joey had to confront Bear as soon as possible because if he was not involved, then he had to make that meeting with Dominick and turn over the money as he had planned. On the other hand, if Bear was in league with Dominick, then he would have no choice but to deal with it the best way possible. At this point, he just wanted this nightmare to end, even if he had to turn himself in to the authorities. He was exhausted from feeling so guilty and deceitful. His mind was made up to do the right thing. It had been a hard lesson, one that would probably put him in jail for many years, but that was a future he had already prepared himself to face.

It sounded and felt like the *Sea Bear* was slowing down, and Joey figured that they were at least four miles out. No land was visible, just water and blue skies. As the boat slowed and eventually stopped slicing through the water, Bear shut off the engines, letting the boat drift with the strong current. Joey heard Bear walking down the steps from the main control bridge and heading straight to the cabin, saying, "You need another drink partner?"

"No, I'm good for now," Joey said.

"You've been too good since I've known you. It's time for you to retire and relax," Bear said as he came out from the cabin with a full drink. He slumped into the chair facing Joey.

"What do you mean?" Joey asked, figuring the booze had taken its full effect.

"You know what I mean. You've been shot, injured on the goddamn job. Take the fucking sixty-six and two-thirds percent pension—it's tax free for Christ's sake. You've earned it." Bear took another healthy gulp of his drink, finishing about a third of the glass.

Joey saw that Bear was getting drunk; even a man Bear's size couldn't withstand that pace. He knew Bear would start cursing when he was drunk, a clue most people weren't aware of. Joey knew he could drink a bottle of scotch and the person Bear was talking with would have no idea he'd been drinking. But today, the cursing started way too early, which was definitely inconvenient. Joey wanted—needed—genuine answers to his questions. He figured that he'd better get started soon.

"I guess you're right. I've put in my time and paid my dues. But for now, I'll let them pay me 100 percent and decide what to do when I'm off of sick leave," Joey said, thinking of a way to change the subject.

"It's your life, and it goes by fast. Take advantage while you can. You never know what lies ahead, do you, Joey?" Bear said as he stared into his glass of scotch.

An uneasy silence hung in the air for a moment, but it seemed to Joey to last noticeably longer than just a few seconds.

Bear looked up at Joey as he came out of his trance, his tone somber as he spoke. "So, pal, what was so urgent that you needed to talk with me?"

Joey got up to grab another beer from the fridge. "Can I get you another scotch, Bear," he yelled.

Bear declined by holding up a glass that still had a little of the gold liquid remaining. Joey sat back down and kept quiet as he wrestled with the words he was going to use. Despite his alcohol-induced melancholy, Bear took the initiative away from Joey.

Using his best Godfather imitation, Bear said, "Now that you have had your drink, tell me what's troubling you."

Joey knew there was no easy way of asking the questions. *If Bear is the good friend I think he is,* Joey thought, *then he should understand why I need to ask.* "You know how bad I felt about Tom getting killed by those scumbags?"

Bear slowly nodded his head as Joey continued.

"When you told me about your FBI friend DeSordi and the traceable money, it gave me hope that they would catch Dominick and his street thugs sooner rather than later. I kept watching the news and waiting. Waiting for you to call with an update, but you didn't." Joey paused and saw that Bear was looking straight at him, not saying a word. "Well, when I didn't hear anything, I thought I'd try to contact Agent DeSordi myself–"

"You what? I told you that in complete confidence, Joe!" Bear yelled. "What the fuck would you do that for?"

"Relax, Bear. I couldn't contact him. In fact, there was no listing in the Newark or New York offices for anyone named DeSordi."

"Is that why you've got a bug up your ass? You called because the FBI operator couldn't hook you up with DeSordi? Why in hell didn't you just call me? I'd have given you his number if it really meant that much to you. You're my friend, not DeSordi. Fuck him and fuck the chief too."

Joey started to feel guilty again about even thinking Bear might be involved in this mess. "I'm sorry, Bear, I haven't been myself lately. I don't know what I was thinking." *If he only knew,* Joey thought.

Joey began to feel his bond for Bear again, realizing that his accusations only served to put a wedge between the two of them. Joey downed his beer, ducked back inside, and came out again holding a Grey Goose on the rocks and a scotch for his friend. He took a big gulp and felt the warmth flow down from his throat to his stomach, waiting for a slight buzz to come next. He knew this was his first and last drink because of his meeting with Dominick.

The sun was beating down hard, and the men moved their chairs into the shade. There was a strong wind coming out of the south, and the boat was drifting at the mercy of the current beneath it. Joey looked over and saw Bear staring at him, smiling.

"I've known you too long, Joey. What else is bothering you? Trust me, whatever it is, I can probably explain it. And if I can't, I can get the answers you need."

"Okay, okay. You do know me too well," Joey said, shaking his head in disbelief. "I sailed down the Navesink River to the Shrewsbury River and noticed your boat was docked at Dominick's house before

I called you." Joey paused a moment to see if there was any change in Bear's demeanor, but he saw none. "Then while you were giving me a tour of the boat, I turned on the TV in the cabin and looked at the six screens that monitor your yacht here."

Bear started to speak, but Joey raised his hand.

"Let me finish, Bear. You want to know what's really bothering me, so I'm telling you. The fact that you said it was a TV and not security cameras isn't what bothered me, it was the room you wouldn't show me. Your storage room. It looked like someone was in there. Why would you lie to your good friend? Whats going on?"

Bear erupted with his loud, deep laugh–a laugh that Joey hadn't heard in a long while. "Is that it? Is that all of it?"

"Yeah. That's it," Joey said, relieved to get it off his chest.

"You know, Joey, I should be very pissed off at you right now. If I'm correct, you think I made up that story about DeSordi and that I'm somehow wrapped up with Dominick Zarza. Maybe you think someone is in that bedroom waiting to kill you." Bear took a sip of his scotch and smiled, not looking or sounding as drunk as he did before. "Am I close? You know, I never could figure out why you didn't become a detective. You'd have made a good one–but not as good as me. So you accuse me of lying, being a drug dealer, and setting you up to be killed. Well, listen carefully, shit for brains. First, Agent Dave DeSordi works out of the Washington DC office on special assignments like the one I told you about. You definitely wouldn't have found him in the Newark or New York offices. Second, what I am about to tell you is strictly between us. Do you get that this time?"

Joey was listening, not missing a word. "Got it."

"You're absolutely right. I was at Dominick's house earlier. Do you know why?"

The only thing Joey could do was sit quietly and shrug his good shoulder.

"Because Ann called me from Dominick's house."

Joey raised his eyebrows.

"That's right, the chief's secretary. She wanted me to pick her up. I don't know if you knew, but they've been going out, dating since last year. They met at an awards dinner."

Joey's mind shot back to Sergeant Sherman's office, the picture on the wall of Kevin, Ann, Dominick, and the chief. The picture had Ann on the right side of Dominick with Reinus the Anus on the left. It looked like they were a couple, or Ann would have been next to the chief.

"Are you with me, Joe?"

"Yes."

"Things started to go bad, I guess, and I believe Ann started to do cocaine with this fat bastard so—"

"You picked her up and that's who's in the bedroom?" Joey said, feeling very relieved.

"That's right, detective Joe. She was out of it when I picked her up, and she went right to sleep. I know she respects you and wouldn't want you to see her like that, so I tried to keep it a secret. But nothing gets by you, Joey," Bear said sarcastically.

"Sorry, Bear, I don't know what to say. Nothing seems to be going right lately."

"Just do the right thing, and everything will fall into place."

"Like being able to afford a boat like this?"

"I worked hard and saved my money. Some people retire and buy beach houses close to the water. I prefer to be on the water. If you had kept your dick in your pants and settled down, you'd be in the same position."

"I don't think it's my lifestyle," Joey said, grinning. "Plus, my ex-wife took all the money."

Bear studied Joey after a moment of silence and said, "You're still not a hundred percent sure, are you, partner?"

"Whatta you mean? Not sure?"

"Like I said, you still have some doubt? So what I'm going to do will definitely clear up any suspicion you might have," Bear said as he took out his cell phone and flipped it open.

"Who you calling?"

"I'm calling Agent DeSordi. I have his direct line. I'll dial the number and give you the phone. If he answers, he'll identify himself, and then hand the phone to me. Once I talk to him, I'll give you the phone—"

"That's not necessary. I believe you. Stop the bullshit!" Joey said, interrupting Bear.

"Nope, I insist," Bear said as he punched in the number and handed the phone to Joey.

On the third ring, the phone was answered. "You have reached the desk of Agent DeSordi, please leave a message and a return number. If this is an emergency, call the Washington DC main office at 401-555-1555." Joey listened and ended the call after the message stopped.

"He wasn't at his desk. I got his voice mail."

"He's a busy guy, you should have left a message with your number," Bear said, enjoying the moment. Watching Joey squirm in his seat.

"Okay, you made your point. I apologize again."

Both men heard a sound from the cabin, which made Joey and Bear look up, and moments later, Ann stood in the doorway. Her eyes were bloodshot, her hair was a mess, and she'd lost a lot of weight. When she saw Joey, she started crying. She lowered her eyes, not able to meet his gaze, and said, "I'm sorry, Joey." The words forced out in between sobs and tears.

"Are you okay, Ann?" Joey asked, getting up from his chair to hold her.

She held out her arms and started to walk toward him and said, "I didn't mean it. I don't know how it all happened."

Bear shot up and grabbed her before Joey could get to her. "Ann, you need to get some rest," Bear said, putting his huge arms around her tiny shoulders and escorting her back inside the cabin to her room.

When Bear returned, he said to Joey, "Ann told me she would call you when she felt better."

Joey nodded in disbelief. "How could this have happened to her?" Joey asked to no one in particular.

"Let's get going. I should get her home and see about getting her into a rehab clinic."

"Good idea. If you need any help, let me know," Joey said as Bear headed to the main console and started the engines.

As Joey watched the wake behind him, it became clear to him how Dominick had learned all of his and Tom's personal information. How he had access to all the police reports. It was Ann. It made sense; she had worked in every department at one time or another and had all the passwords for all the computers. She probably lost herself in the money and drugs and became addicted to cocaine. She probably did whatever Dominick wanted in return for a hit of coke. Maybe Bear was right. Retirement sounds like a good idea. *When this nightmare is finally over, I will go to Florida and see my mother on a sixty-six and two-thirds percent tax-free pension,* he thought.

Chapter 21

Bear DROPPED JOEY off at Barnacle Bill's and said he was going to the Salt Creek for lunch. It was clearly an open invitation, but Joey declined by saying he had an appointment, which he certainly did.

Joey had forty-five minutes before his meeting with Dominick, and he still had to get the money. Since they ransacked his boat, and he'd learned that the money could be traced, he'd hidden it in a waterproof bag by Pirate's Cove, near the pier. The only thing he had to do was get it. Afterward, he'd meet Dominick, Ziggy, and TJ by boat and have one of them wire the hundred fifty large to his offshore account. In return, Joey would give them their million two—and he'd be glad to be rid of it. Joey sailed his boat to Pirate's Cove, keeping a sharp eye out for any of Dominick's boats. Fortunately, the only ones he saw were those that belonged to the weekenders, who were water-skiing with their twenty-foot boats, their squadrons of wave runners zigzagging across the water. Every time a wave runner came close, Joey raised his guard. He knew it wouldn't be difficult to spot Ziggy or TJ. Even in light of his situation, Joey smiled to himself, envisioning them both zigzagging through the water with no shirts, just gold chains around their necks, and a shoulder holster packed with a gun.

Joey sat in his sailboat next to the pier with the money. Forty-five minutes had passed, and there was no sign of Dominick. He gave it another thirty minutes, but still no one showed up. *Were they planning some type of attack? Did they get the time mixed up?* He dialed the cell number Ziggy had given him, but it was disconnected. Another half hour later, Joey was certain that Dominick was not going to show. He wanted the nightmare to end, wanted to give Dominick the money so there would be no more trouble and no more threats. The money had caused him enough trouble to last a lifetime, and he was going to get rid of it no matter what. He had to. Let Dominick and his cronies go to prison; they deserved it. Instead of mailing Anus the Reinus the $50,000, he would mail it to Ann's house. Let her get busted for what she had done to him and his partner.

Finally tired of waiting, Joey decided he would go to Dominick's house and give him the money. He knew it would be much more dangerous, but it had to be done. He pulled up the anchor and started to motor slowly to the Shrewsbury River toward Dominick's house. As he cruised along the peninsula and rounded the tip toward the channel, he saw the *Sea Bear* coming in his direction. He could see Bear up in Seagull's Nest waving to him. As the boats grew closer, Joey heard Bear yelling for him to come alongside. Joey slowed as much as he could while Bear maneuvered his boat effortlessly, close enough that the boats were nearly touching.

Bear came down from the bridge and threw over several fenders so the boats wouldn't mar each other. "Tie one of your lines to my boat, and I'll secure a line at the bow," Bear yelled to Joey. He hesitated but did so against his better judgment. Joey figured that he insulted Bear with his accusations and felt that he could at least give him a couple more minutes of his time. After all, Dominick wasn't watching the clock, so why should he? Once he and Bear had secured the lines, Bear came to the portside.

"Come aboard, Joe. There's something I forgot to tell you, and I rather tell you in person."

Joey climbed up, and Bear gestured for him to come inside the cabin. Joey entered the cabin, and Bear slid the door closed.

"Too hot out there. It's better if we sit in the air-conditioning," Bear said, taking a seat on the other side of the cabin.

"So what's up?" Joey said, sensing the urgency in Bear's demeanor. He looked like he was on edge, but the captain of the *Sea Bear* seemed perfectly sober. *If he went to eat,* Joey thought, *he must not have had anything to drink.* Knowing Bear, that would be impossible.

Bear looked straight into Joey's eyes. "Dominick isn't coming. I'm here for the money. It's mine, and I want it."

Joey felt the knot in his stomach begin to tighten again, not because of the surprise, but from the disappointment. He was disappointed and disgusted with himself, with his so-called friend Bear and even with Ann. Nobody was innocent; all were responsible for killing his partner. The police, who were supposed to serve and protect the public, had become worse than the criminals they arrested. And Joey knew he was just as guilty.

"I thought the money was Dominick's?" Joey said as he discreetly pushed a button on the side of the small rectangular box in his pants pocket.

"Dominick had the money and influence, but only by name. The Zarza name still carries a lot of weight in this town. It became just too hard for me to resist getting a piece of the action, especially since I'm in charge of narcotics. It was a great setup, untouchable until you came along and took the money."

Joey could not believe what he was hearing. He certainly saw the man who stood in front of him, but Joey no longer knew who he was. He sounded desperate, definitely not a captain on the Two River Police Department who made a six-figure income.

"Why, Bear? Just tell me why."

"It all happened so fast," he started. "About a year ago, I started having money problems with some investments that went bad, lost most of my savings. Then I caught my wife having an affair with my neighbor. She told me she wanted a divorce. My life was falling apart. My son's college tuition was sixty thousand a year, and to top it off, he was arrested for selling amphetamines. I had to pay a lawyer a hundred fifty thousand dollars just to keep him out of jail. I was broke and losing my house. Every dollar I made went to pay bills. I was sinking fast. I didn't want the department to find out, so I did what I had to do."

"You became a fucking drug dealer, Bear! Why didn't you come to me? I would have helped you," Joey yelled.

"I was too embarrassed, Joe. Twenty years on the force, and nothing to show for it. Just as my life was supposed to get comfortable with a good pension and no debt, I was about to be homeless. So one day, one of my detectives busts a local drug dealer who says he wants to make a deal. He tells me that one of his buyers is Dominick Zarza, and I think, wow, what a bust that would be. So I make this guy an informant and keep it to myself. I figured the guy was bullshitting me, but I wanted to find out the truth. A month later, I'm attending the honorary PBA dinner and sitting with the chief, Ann, Captain Grahill, his wife, and Dominick. I'm looking at Dominick all night, and I knew he was doing coke. He kept leaving the table, never ate dinner, and had a runny red nose. I couldn't believe he was doing cocaine at a police function sitting with all us cops. Then after dinner, he invites me, the chief, and Ann to his mansion. What a house. It was unbelievable. The grounds, the view, the maids, butlers, yachts docked on his private pier. I drank enough scotch to kill two people. I was very drunk on scotch, and Dominick was high on cocaine. I was desperate, losing my house. I looked around and saw all this wealth. Dominick talked about his new business and said I would make a great partner. He said I could make a mill in just one year with no effort. I knew it was drugs, but I needed the money. I figured one year with Dominick and I'd get out. I had found out that night that he had been dating Ann. Everything just sounded too easy. So Ann became my eyes and ears in the mansion, and the rest is history. I had him hire the drug dealers that we busted. I kept them as informants, letting them know that I could send them to jail anytime I wanted if they failed to cooperate. Even though he lost most of his money in the stock market, Dominick still had a couple of million, but he needed a hundred thousand a month just to maintain his lifestyle. So I ran the business, and we split the money fifty-fifty. Dominick was a pussy. He never could have kept those drug dealers in line if it hadn't been for me. He sat around like the Godfather thinking he gave out the orders, but I was always in the background making sure they did what they were told. I–"

"So you paid off some bills, kept your son out of jail, and bought a big boat so no one would ever think you were broke," Joey said as he pushed the off button on the box in his pocket.

"That's right."

"And in doing so, you had my partner killed. You knew one of us had the money, which is why you gave me that shit story about the traceable money and FBI Agent DeSordi. What did you do, get Desordi's number out of the FBI directory?"

"Nope, I know him. DeSordi is investigating Zarza's bad stock deal. The FBI is trying to locate Keats for insider trading."

"You gambled on calling DeSordi. Hoping he wouldn't answer the phone."

"I knew I'd get his voice mail, he never answers that phone." Bear paused and then continued, "Sorry about your partner. That wasn't supposed to happen."

"Not supposed to happen?" Joey yelled. He'd heard enough. "Fuck you, Bear. You piece of shit! You killed my partner. I'll never give you that money. I hate that money! I'm turning it in, along with myself. You do whatever the fuck you want."

"Joey, I need that money. I've gotta have it!"

Joey stared at Bear, his eyes as black as coal. "I'm leaving with the money and going to headquarters to turn myself in, Bear. I suggest you do the same."

As he turned to leave, he heard the very familiar sound of a round being chambered into a semiautomatic handgun. Joey stopped dead in his tracks and turned to face Bear, who was pointing a forty-five straight at him.

"Sorry, Joe. You're not leaving until I get the money. How hypocritical have you gotten? You think you're better than me? You took the money, and now you want to make everything better by turning yourself in. Waa, waa, waa."

"If I don't, I won't be able to live with myself," Joey said, taking a step back.

"I need that money. Just give it to me and you can walk away. I'll take care of everything else," Bear said. He held the pistol firmly in a hand that was rock steady. "Too late, Bear. It's time you stopped hiding behind the blue. I'm done, and so are you." Joey lifted both hands. "I'm going into my right pocket. It's not a gun."

"Do it very slowly," Bear instructed, the gun pointed at Joey's chest.

Joey reached in his pocket, pulled out a miniature tape recorder, and played back part of their conversation.

Bear became frantic, desperate as Joey turned and started to walk toward the cabin door. Bear shouted, "Don't turn your back on me. Don't leave this boat, Joey. I mean it." His voice getting louder with each syllable.

As Joey reached the door, a gun went off, and the sound inside the cabin deafening. Joey's knees buckled, sure that his body would become limp and hit the floor. But somehow, he was still standing. He turned around slowly to see Ann holding a pistol with Bear lying on the floor in a growing puddle of blood. Ann stood there in shock, still holding Bear's off-duty five-shot chief special in her right hand and crying.

"I'm so sorry, Joey, I'm so sorry." Without warning, she raised the gun to her head and pulled the trigger.

Joey called 911.

Chapter 22

JOEY EXPLAINED TO the police how Captain Whitman was in financial trouble, his son was in trouble, and his wife was going to leave him. The Captain had called him wanting desperately to talk to him. Joey further stated that he had no idea why Ann was on the boat, but that he thought they might have been having an affair. The chief wanted the matter closed as soon as possible and with the least amount of publicity. The incident was buried almost instantly.

Chapter 23

TWO DAYS LATER, Joey took the money to Dominick's house. He didn't see much point in going to jail if he didn't have to. Instead, he'd simply return the money to Dominick, retire to Florida, and suffer the memory of his partner for the rest of his life. Dominick would get a million dollars, and the rest would go to Tom's wife.

As he drove up to Dominick's security entrance, the gates were already opened. He drove past the gates, up the winding road and parked near the majestic front doors of the mansion. He grabbed the bag of money and walked to the front door. Several cars were parked in front of the garages, mostly work vans, but none that he had ever seen before. He rang the doorbell and heard the loud echo on the other side of the huge wooden doors. Several moments later, the door was opened by the elderly gray-haired gentleman he met the first time he was there. The man who peacefully stood behind Dominick while he spoke to him about transferring the money. Joey saw no sign that anyone else was there to meet him, frisk him, or make his life miserable in some other way. Joey walked inside and noticed that the house had changed completely. People were inside cleaning the marble floors and restoring everything to its original beauty.

The old man recognized him immediately. "You are Officer Sabba. Please come in."

Joey entered, carrying the bag of money over his shoulder.

"Follow me."

Joey followed, trying to figure out what was going on. All he wanted to do was return the money and leave—and have no problems with Dominick or his drug dealers. Joey followed the man into a huge study, which could have been the room in which he first met Dominick, but he was unsure. The place had changed so much since his last visit; he barely recognized it. As Joey entered, the man closed the doors behind them.

"Officer Sabba, please have a seat. Is there anything I can get for you? A drink maybe?" the man said very calmly and politely.

"What's your name?" Joey asked.

"My name is Sergio, Officer Sabba, and I know why you're here," he said.

"You do?" Joey asked, dropping the bag of money on the floor.

"Yes, I do. So let me speak so that we understand each other perfectly."

Joey nodded wordlessly.

"I am Dominick's godfather. His father, Raffio, was a dear friend of mine, and I promised him that I would always take care of Dominick no matter what. Raffio was a very smart man who knew his son's limitations. So after leaving him with close to a billion dollars, he also left a five hundred million-dollar trust fund that was kept secret from Dominick. I did my best, but Dominick thought he could be like his father and double the family fortune. As you've seen"–the man waved his arm in a broad arc to indicate the changed condition of the room–"things went wrong. I also know what happened to Captain Whitman and Ann. What a shame. However, I am very familiar with the concept that money can bring out the worst even in the best people. Because of that, I don't hold judgment on anyone, including you. Dominick is currently out of the country undergoing some needed rehabilitation, and I expect you to keep this to yourself as you are in no position to talk. The million dollars that started everything is yours. When Dominick returns home, he will get back into real estate with a half billion dollars, so I wouldn't worry about him."

"What about the others?" Joey asked.

"They are all gone too. You have no idea what the very wealthy can buy."

"You know, I was starting to like you and respect your Italian position. But I think you believe money puts you and your godson above the law."

"Money has always separated the classes, Officer Sabba. Dominick will get healthier and will eventually donate a million dollars to the PBA. Eventually, he'll become the most liked businessman in town. That's just the way it works, Officer. So you can take your million and leave."

Joey's blood started to boil. The arrogance of this bastard! As he did on the *Sea Bear*, Joey fished into his pocket and came up with the tiny tape recorder. As it played, Bear explained how he became partners with Dominick. The godfather standing in front of him listened carefully.

"I don't care how much money Dominick has, this tape will put him away for years," Joey said.

"What do you want?"

"I thought you knew, you self-righteous bastard. I came here to return the money to Dominick to make up for what I have done."

The godfather sat down in front of a desk, pulled open a drawer, and took out a checkbook. He scribbled down a number and handed it to Joey.

Joey looked at the check doing his best to look unimpressed, but the damn thing had too many zeros. Three million dollars carries a lot of weight.

Joey picked up the tape recorder along with the check. "When this check clears, I'll destroy the tape."

The small man smiled ever so slightly. "I don't think you quite understand, Officer Sabba. If that tape were ever to become public, your life and those of all your loved ones would be forfeit. Think about something terribly frightening and then multiply that by, say, a hundred. Dominick is my loved one, and I will see to it that nothing happens to him. That check is not intended to keep you quiet, instead, you may consider it a going-away present."

The old man straightened his blazer jacket, careful to maintain an impeccable appearance. "As you can see, I am very busy getting the house in order—"

"What happened to the others?" Joey asked a second time.

"They all have been dismissed. None of them will ever be seen in this house again. Take that for what it's worth. I must be going now, Officer. Our business is over. Permanently."

Seemingly out of nowhere, a well-dressed butler padded into the room.

"See this gentleman to the door, please," Sergio said, his voice devoid of emotion. Immediately after, the old man walked across the room and left through a door on the other side.

Chapter 24

THREE WEEKS HAD passed. Joey had exactly a million two in cash and another three million in a check that had already cleared and was resting comfortably in his offshore account. He had submitted his retirement papers to the department, which they processed almost immediately. Joey sold his sailboat and had his condo up for sale and had given most of his belongings to Tommy's wife. He established a million-dollar trust fund for her two kids and headed out to Florida to live by his mother.

Joey finished packing at about seven in the evening, loading his car with nothing other than a few bottles of water and the bag of money, which he kept on the floor in front of the rear passenger's seat. He had enough money to buy whatever he wanted along the way. It was nearly eight thirty when Joey finally left his condo to start his trip to Florida. He had the radio blasting, and his thoughts were on nothing else but the future.

As he drove down Route 88 across Two River toward the parkway, he came upon that same dangerous curve. As he slowed and began to snake around the sharp curve, he was blinded by a pair of headlights that appeared to be coming straight at him. The drunk driver speeding toward him made no attempt to stop, and a second later, there was a huge flash of light. Both drivers were killed instantly.

The police responded, and the first officer on the scene opened the front door of Joey's car and saw instantly that he was dead. He then pulled open the rear door and saw a bundle of wrapped hundred-dollar bills that had spilled from a canvas bag behind the driver's seat.

"Hmmm." He smiled to himself.